ALMOST ROMANCE

KYLIE GILMORE

Cover design by Sweet 'N Spicy Designs

Published by: Extra Fancy Books

ISBN-13: 978-1-942238-19-5

Because love isn't a science…

1

Kate Lewis piled her plate with red, green, and blue artificially colored mini cheese balls at the University of Chicago's physics department holiday party while calculating how much longer she had to pretend to be merry. She was dying to take off these awful pantyhose, go to the lab, and get back to work. Someone cranked up the Bare Naked Ladies' holiday CD, and she relaxed marginally.

The department's secretary had draped silver garland along the ceiling in an attempt to make the normally sterile meeting room feel festive. The long meeting table had been pushed to the side to hold the hors d'oeuvres, with a small artificial tree at one end of the table and a menorah with fake candles at the other end. The chairs were gone, which just made all the physicists cling to the periphery of the room. She could develop a theory of molecular party dynamics, but she'd much rather get back to the real work of particle physics.

"I heard the pigs in blankets are good," a familiar masculine voice said.

She whirled and mini cheese balls scattered everywhere. "Ian! What're you doing here?"

She immediately dropped to the floor to pick up the mess and hide the fact that she was in the throes of a full-on body blush. Ian Furnukle, the man who rid her of her damn virginity four years ago, knelt at her side to help. He wore a black sweater, khakis, and black Adidas sneakers. His scent was woodsy with a hint of citrus that she knew was his cologne, but it still worked like a cool breeze after a rain shower. Dammit! Her thoughts always went squirrely when Ian was around. He had the worst possible timing. He was not supposed to be here in Chicago. Last she'd heard he was working in Boston.

His wavy brown hair fell over one eye, and he pushed it away. "Hi, Kate."

"Hi!" she squeaked. "Why are you here?" Kate didn't do surprises well.

He was so close it felt like he was about to kiss her. Her heart was racing. He hadn't shaved. Last time she'd seen him he was clean-shaven, and she'd missed the stubble. She pushed her large tortoiseshell glasses back in place with a shaky hand and met his warm brown eyes.

He gave her a lopsided smile. "I'm in consulting. Picked up the physics lab as a client."

Ian had a PhD in computer science and worked wherever hard-core computer applications were needed. It wasn't out of the realm of possibility that he might be needed in a lab with heavy data-analysis requirements. Still, she was a little pissed her older sister, Amber, hadn't mentioned Ian was in Chicago. She always knew the basics on Ian's life on account of Amber being married to Ian's older brother Barry.

He finished piling the cheese balls on the plate, stood,

and tossed it in the trash. By the time he returned to her side, she was standing in a composed, confident way.

She reached out and shook his hand in a hearty gesture, ignoring the hot tingles the touch produced. "Ian, it was very nice to see you. I must be going now."

"Am I making you nervous?"

Her speech always became more formal when she was nervous. It was an unfortunate fallback to her formal upbringing. Despite the fact that she'd only seen Ian on and off over the past four years, the one summer they'd spent together had been deeply intimate. No one ever understood her better than Ian.

"Of course not." She smoothed her flyaway blond hair and checked to be sure it was still in the loose bun she'd made this morning. Mostly still in a bun. "Don't be ridiculous," she added for good measure.

Now she felt like she couldn't leave or it would confirm Ian's theory of his proximity making her nervous. She stood there, unsure what to do with her hands. As if this holiday party hadn't been awkward enough with a bunch of physicists standing around pretending to have a good time. She put a hand on her hip and went for party casual. Ian was a bit of a wildcard in her life. They were thrown together at random intervals due to the married-siblings connection. The last time she'd seen him—approximately seven months ago—had been…overstimulating.

Ian shoved his hands in his pockets. "How ya been, Kate? You like Chicago?"

"It's met my expectations. And how are you?"

He lifted one shoulder up and down. "Can't complain."

She'd caved to societal expectations and worn a dark green holiday dress that she was now secretly grateful for because it made her look more like a woman with curves than her usual uniform of baggy sweater and faded jeans. Not that she cared about looking good in front of Ian. It wasn't like he was her boyfriend. Woo! She'd love to escape to the ladies' room and take off these pantyhose that had a stranglehold on her waist and were heating other unmentionable areas due to the extra layer. Definitely not because of Ian, she reassured herself, the man hadn't even touched her.

She glanced at the clock on the wall, certain that the level of her anxiety must mean she'd been away from the lab long enough. Thirty-three minutes. That definitely counted as making an appearance and having a good time. Several of her colleagues were gathered around Nate's overly large cell phone. He was probably showing off another podcast he enjoyed about murderers. The men's taste in entertainment did not mesh with hers. She was the only woman in the particle physics lab, where she was approximately seven months into a two-year postdoctorate fellowship. Her PhD was in experimental nuclear and particle physics. Not that she would've been BFFs with another woman if they happened to be there. It was like throwing two lions together. You might hope they'd bond or mate or whatever, but it would be a completely random event based on factors that she'd yet to grasp in female relationships. Her sister, Amber, seven years older, was much better at all that stuff and had advised Kate over the years. Amber was Kate's best friend. Not that she'd ever told her sister that. Some things were better left unsaid.

Ian's scent wafted over her, and she realized with a start that he was now within her personal space, which meant he intended to do something physical. An involuntary hot tingle of anticipation rushed through her. Sure enough, he snagged her hand and pulled her to an unoccupied corner of the room. She snatched her hand back. She couldn't have her colleagues see her holding hands with Ian. They'd get the wrong idea. So would he.

So would her body.

Ian always brought out her slutty side.

He pushed a strand of hair away from her face. "Did you get the flowers? Why didn't you return my calls or texts?"

Their timing had always been bad. The first time they'd hooked up, as she'd explained to him when she was twenty-one, she was too young to settle down and needed to explore other male possibilities. Ian had eventually moved on to a committed relationship with a fellow computer scientist for three years, taking him off the market. That ended when the woman gave him an ultimatum—marry her or she'd walk. Ian let her walk. Kate bit back a sigh. It was regrettable that Ian had hooked up with Kate a second time when she was at the settling-down age of twenty-five because it was right before she had to move to Chicago.

"I didn't want to encourage you," she said. "Excuse me. I'm very thirsty."

She headed back to the long table with a variety of festive hors d'oeuvres she'd yet to try and grabbed a plastic cup by the punch bowl. She hoped no one had spiked it because she didn't want to get too crazy with Ian around. Her embarrassing lack of control around him was a serious character flaw. She could feel his heat at her back, which meant he was too close.

She spoke over her shoulder. "This was exactly the problem four years ago. You acted like a lovesick—ah!" The plastic cup went flying as he yanked her behind a potted plant. Luckily, she hadn't filled the cup yet. Some heads turned in their direction.

"What are you doing?" she exclaimed.

One corner of his mouth lifted. "I wanted some privacy."

"I wouldn't call standing behind a ficus tree private." She gestured to the leaves. "There are gaps in the foliage."

Ian lowered his voice. "I still think about that night."

She froze.

"Do you?"

She stared straight ahead. "I think about a lot of things." She really tried not to think about that night. It only served to crank up her libido, which was pointless because Ian was in Boston, and she was in Chicago. Fantasizing about things she couldn't have was a waste of her brain power. She needed all of her focus for work. She reminded herself of that whenever she found herself daydreaming about…that night.

She occasionally dreamt about it too, waking in a hot, aching state of near orgasm. One stroke could push her over the edge. She crossed her arms, trying to appear dignified even as heat pooled between her legs.

He leaned down to her ear. "All three times." Ian was six foot to her five foot two and often had to lean down to her ear. Just not this close, usually. She could feel her body softening, which was entirely inappropriate for a physics holiday party. Yes, they'd had sex a grand total of three times, but she knew "that night" that he referred to had to be the most recent time because it was, unfortunately, stuck in her brain too. She'd left in a hurry right after.

"It was only one time," she said. One mind-blowing, paradigm-shifting time.

His low voice was so close to her ear that the sound waves sent hot tingling vibrations through her, which made no sense as sound waves at this decibel did *not* produce heat. "Twice to make sure you weren't a virgin."

Her cheeks burned. "And once to celebrate your graduation."

Ian had unexpectedly made an appearance at her PhD graduation from MIT last May, tagging along with his brother and Amber. He convinced her to celebrate that night with a beer. He knew beer made her lusty.

She uncrossed her arms and met his heated gaze. "Ian, this is an inappropriate conversation for a holiday party."

"Show me your lab."

She didn't move.

His voice dropped to a low, scraping register that made her stomach flutter. "And then tell me all about your research in great detail."

She swallowed hard. She had to be firm with Ian because he was entirely too good at turning her on. Which was a very bad idea given her current situation. "You don't want to hear about that." She crossed her arms again, working on not melting. "You're trying to seduce me."

She stepped out from behind the plant. Ian grabbed her hand and pulled her out into the hallway. "Which way?" he asked.

"Left," she said automatically. She pulled her hand from his warm grip and relaxed considerably now that she wasn't stuck in the artificially festive meeting room. The hallway was cooler temperature-wise on account of less bodies, and Ian had finally gotten the message that she needed a little more space.

"Are you working on the particle accelerator?" Ian asked as they walked.

Now she was on familiar, confident ground. "Yes."

"Any publishable results?"

"I just had a paper accepted into *The Journal of Experimental and Particle Physics* on a direct measurement of the total decay width of the top quark." She stopped in front of the door and gestured to where the huge particle accelerator was located. "This is it."

He peered inside and whistled under his breath. He turned back to her. "Show me your office too."

That worked for her. She had a comfortable baggy sweater and broken-in jeans stashed in there for after the party. She did an about-face and led the way to the building next door. The cold winter air felt bracing and refreshing on their short walk over. Ian followed her into her small windowless office with a desk, computer, and file cabinet. The walls were plain white, and the floor a dingy speckled linoleum that always reminded her of scattered photons. The only personal touch was an original watercolor hanging on the wall across from her desk of a dragon breathing out a pink cloud. It was a graduation gift from Amber, who was an amazing watercolor artist. The painting inspired her to expand her imagination when lost in equations, to look for new and different ways to explain the universe.

She turned, about to ask Ian to give her a moment to change, when the room went dark. "Ian! Turn the lights back on."

The door clicked shut. "Not until you answer a few questions."

She considered if she could maneuver in the dark to the desk drawer where she'd stashed her purse with its handy flashlight keychain. But then Ian held both of her hands in his warm grip, which somehow warmed her all over. "Okay, what?" she asked.

"How many men have you slept with in the last four years?" While the question was intimate, it was within the normal realm of their conversations. They talked about anything and everything. Ian had been very helpful in explaining things of a sexual nature early on, before she was experienced. Still, this conversation could easily become foreplay, especially in the private darkness of her office. Ian was quite the dirty talker, capable of accelerating her libido at an alarmingly high rate.

"You're not my boyfriend," she said. "You don't get to ask me questions about my sexual history."

His thumb stroked across the sensitive underside of her wrist, making her pulse skitter. "Counting me."

She sucked in a breath. "I fail to see the relevance of this question."

"That many, huh? Twenty, thirty?"

"No! Five!" She really couldn't tolerate inaccuracies, especially in numbers. Like nails on the chalkboard for her.

He squeezed her hands gently. "Five. Including me. Did you sow your wild oats, Kate?" She could hear the smile in his voice, which annoyed her because his number before his big relationship was probably much higher.

"I guess." She'd told him she'd wanted to sow her wild oats in grad school after their first hookup, but truthfully the men she'd been with had been rather disappointing. None of them had given her the full-tilt boogie orgasm she'd hoped for, which would've made them a ten on her rating system. Ian had explained about the full-tilt boogie once when she was a virgin and dying not to be. The topic came up naturally when they'd overheard the screams of ecstasy from across the hall where their respective siblings, Amber and Barry, were fucking like rabbits. She and Ian were often kicked out of the apartment for their siblings' naked time and hung out a lot that one summer because of it.

"And how would you rate those other men on your

performance scale of one to ten?" Ian asked, entwining his fingers with hers. "Ten being full-tilt boogie."

She flushed and yanked her hands out of his grasp. "Ian, this conversation is over." The way he intuitively knew what was in her head was unnerving. Especially since she always had to guess, usually incorrectly, what was going on in someone else's head. She carefully skirted her way around him and turned the light back on. She blinked owlishly.

"That bad, huh?" he asked. "Only threes or fours, or, ooh—" his voice took on a pitying tone "—pathetic *ones*?"

"Not at all! The median was seven point two."

He leaned close and spoke the next words near her ear, his breath hot across her skin, making her knees weak. "And what was I?"

She squirmed because the truth was only going to get her in deeper. She clung to a technicality. If she discarded the outlier, the graduation beer-driven hookup, and focused on the deflowering, she had a good answer. "I had nothing to compare you to, so no relevant scale or scoring system was applicable."

He pulled back and met her eyes. "Ten?"

"A solid eight." She was forced to admit that for the sake of accuracy.

He cocked his head. "Why not a ten?"

"A ten requires things you couldn't be expected to do with a virgin in terms of stimulation or erotic..." She trailed off at the heated look in his eyes, feeling like somehow the conversation had gotten away from her. She fanned herself, suddenly overheated. "I wish I had a window." A nice cold winter breeze would be awesome.

He leaned closer, and her body temperature spiked again. It was so inconvenient the way he took her from a nice comfortable state of rest to full thrusters ahead. "You're forgetting the last time we were together."

That was definitely a ten, but she did *not* want to encourage him. For a very legitimate reason. That she would tell him as soon as she found out how she rated.

"What's your rating for all the women you slept with?" she asked casually.

His brown eyes twinkled with amusement. "You get a ten, even the first time."

"Oh!" She tittered. "A ten! I—you flatter me." She giggled in a very uncharacteristic way and smoothed her hair. "I was so inexperienced. I didn't even know what I was doing."

"You were open and honest, and you let me do whatever I wanted." His fingers slid into her hair, cradling her head with one large hand. Her breath caught, but she couldn't seem to move away. "And I realized sex is only special with the right person. Kate, you're that right person for me."

"Ian," she said nervously, "I-I don't know why you'd say that. I was a dopey desperate virgin. And that last time I was drunk."

"No, you were tipsy from one beer." His mouth grazed her earlobe as he spoke in a low, husky voice. "And the virgin thing, well, it was a privilege to be your first."

She shivered. "Oh."

He pulled back, his eyes hot on hers. "I'm going to kiss you now."

"In my office?" she asked inanely.

"In your office," he confirmed.

"Why?" she asked softly in a voice that sounded like an invitation even to her ears. This was a very bad idea. But his hand was so warm and large and strong, tipping her head back in delicious anticipation. And he smelled so good.

"Wrong question." His gaze dropped to her mouth. "Ask how long I'll be kissing you."

"Ian," she breathed.

His arm wrapped around her waist and with a quick tug made her tip into him. "Until you agree to let me give you a ten."

She melted against the heat and strength of his body, but even so, a voice in her head was shouting at her to protest. There was a small problem with this line of experimentation. "Ian—"

She was cut off when his lips met hers, hot and demanding, and that electrifying chemistry that always happened when he kissed her shot straight through her body, making her mind shut down, a blissful break from its usual constant cranking. Only Ian could make her forget the world and lose herself in the moment. She clutched his sweater as he palmed her ass and pulled her up on tiptoe, pressed against his long, lean body. The kiss went on and on, and she just let go, lost in the feel of his mouth claiming hers, his taste, his scent. Nothing mattered except this heat that consumed her, made her ache and remember what they had together.

He lifted his head just as she attempted to climb his body, one leg lifted and wrapped around his. He gazed into her eyes with a warm smile. "Let's go."

She set her leg down and released her hold on his sweater, smoothing it back in place. And then she was forced to admit a very unfortunate fact that just proved her theory that their timing would never be right. "I have a boyfriend."

2
___

Four years ago…

Kate was a desperately horny twenty-one-year-old virgin. And she was determined to change that status tonight. It really wasn't fair that she'd spent the last seven weeks listening to her older sister, Amber, get it on with her boyfriend, Barry. She didn't want to listen. They'd get busy at the drop of a hat, and she could barely get out of the apartment fast enough. She was spending the summer between college and grad school at her sister's place. And, right across the hall, was an eligible, experienced twenty-four-year-old *man*.

Ian was much more of a man than any of the boys she went to college with in her brief three years on campus. He was tall with broad shoulders and large hands that she desperately wanted on her. Not only that, he had a deep, masculine voice, a regular five o'clock shadow, and an easygoing confidence that told her he'd know what to do in the bedroom. Also, Amber had told her Ian was a player and had slept with many women in the computer science, physics, and engineering departments of MIT. That meant she was his type, and he'd know exactly what to do with a woman like her. The problem was, Ian was Barry's younger brother, staying at Barry's apartment for the summer, and that made him off-limits. According to Amber. And Barry. No one wanted the player Ian to touch the innocent Kate, except Kate herself.

The first time they'd hung out, while their siblings burned up the sheets, she'd told him she was saving herself for marriage because she didn't want him to think she was a total inexperienced dork for no good reason. He'd said he respected that. He offered her a beer and they sat together on the sofa, watching the Sox game and talking. At least he watched the Sox game, she watched him. She'd never hung out with an older, good-looking man before and surreptitiously checked him out. He was lean with wavy brown hair that often fell over one eye. His eyes were a deep brown. He had a stubbled jaw that she wanted to feel, just to stroke it, a quick smile, and a mellow demeanor that made her relax and feel like she might actually be cool enough to hang with him. And he was so smart too, halfway to a PhD in computer science, which was just as big of a turn-on for her. The brains and the manliness made him the total package.

They talked about math and computers that first night, and she was feeling so tipsy and, yes, lusty from the beer. She never drank beer in college because she was too busy studying. She'd completed a double major in math and physics with top honors in three years.

Ian kept smiling at her as they talked. Her libido cranked higher. She finished her second beer, her hormones at an all-time buzzing high. She pulled the band out of her hair, shook out her usual bun, and finally made her move, putting her hand on his upper thigh and stroking inward. She'd seen the move before in a movie.

His head snapped away from the TV to her, his brown eyes wide. And then he put his large hand on hers and held it still.

"Do you want to do something?" she asked, unsure how to phrase her request to please take her virginity.

He looked at her quite seriously and for a moment her hopes soared. Then he gave her hand a little squeeze and moved it off his leg. "I respect you too much to…do something."

"You can!"

His lips formed a grim line. "That's the beer talking. I know you're saving yourself. So, thank you, but no, thank you." He went back to watching the game, and she sat there, completely mortified and on the edge of tears. She never, ever cried. Finally, she couldn't take the humiliation of his rejection anymore and rushed back across the hall to the safety of her sister's apartment.

"Hey, where're you going?" he called. "The game's not over!"

She'd cried all over her sister, who'd reassured her that she'd find someone special one day, and then took her shopping for clothes that would make her more appealing to the opposite sex. Because, according to Amber, Kate's usual oversized, baggy T-shirts and frayed jeans were hiding her body. Right away her new clothes—halter tops and short skirts—had Ian's attention. But she'd been hurt by his rejection and ignored him at first. He'd backed off and went back to being friendly, which was *not* the intended effect. She resorted to wearing her sister's summer pajamas, which were practically see-through (short-sleeve top with shorts) with no underwear. And while she knew she had his attention, Ian was frustratingly still acting like they were just friends hanging out. Seven weeks getting to know Ian as a friend had been enough for her to know two things: 1) she trusted him implicitly, and 2) she heated wherever they accidentally touched. That was plenty. There would be no better candidate. There would be no better time.

When Kate had returned to the apartment late on the night soon to be thought of as The Deflowering, after spending the evening browsing at a nearby bookstore, she'd discovered Amber had returned early and was sound asleep. That meant there was no one to stop Kate and try to talk her out of it. Kate had even peeked into her sister's room to be sure Amber was asleep. She snagged her sister's pink satin robe and returned to the living room. Then she texted Ian that she wanted to hang out. He replied: *come on over*. She texted back one more time inquiring where Barry was because he wasn't with Amber and the last thing she needed was him seeing what Ian was about to see.

He's sleeping, he texted back.

It was strange that Amber and Barry had gone to sleep separately, early even, but she didn't spend any time thinking about it because she was about to cross over into the world of pleasure. She quickly stripped down naked, put on the robe, and shook out her hair. She left her glasses behind and hoped she could get from point A to point B successfully without slamming into anything sharp or pointy. She could only see things that were very close, as she hoped Ian would be for the remainder of the evening.

She quietly left the apartment, went across the hall, and gently knocked. Ian answered the door and gave her his adorable lopsided smile. "Hey."

"Hi." She stepped inside and dropped the robe. "Take me, Ian."

His jaw dropped, and then he grabbed the robe and covered her up, holding it in front of her, pinned to her shoulders in a tight grip. "I thought you were saving yourself."

He was close enough that she could actually see the stubble along his jaw. She desperately wanted him to kiss her, to feel that rough scraping against her.

She lifted her chin. "I'm not."

His eyes searched hers. "Why did you say you were before?" Still not making any move toward her.

Her confidence plummeted, and she reluctantly admitted, "Because I didn't want you to know that nobody wanted me because I'm not..." She swallowed hard. "... beautiful." She knew she wasn't. She was just a nerdy girl with messy hair and glasses and zero fashion sense. A tear escaped and then Ian released his grip on her shoulders, the robe dropped to the floor, and his arms wrapped around her. She sank into his embrace.

"That's a damn lie," he said. "You are beautiful." He wiped the tear on her cheek, and then he kissed her. His large warm hands cradled her face as the kiss got deeper and a fire ignited between them. Her mind went shockingly blank for the first time ever as his mouth claimed hers. He nipped her bottom lip, which made her gasp, and his tongue thrust inside. She'd never been kissed like this in her life. She clutched his shirt for balance because her knees were weak. His hands were stroking all over her body, her shoulders, down her arms, her hips, her sides, and finally stopping to cup her breasts. She moaned as he stroked his thumbs across her nipples.

"Kate," he growled, leaning down to taste and suckle one hard nipple into his mouth.

Heat flooded her. She was ready, way past ready. She

tangled her hand in his hair. "Please, Ian, hurry up and take me." She pulled at his shirt, and he took it off.

He kissed her again. "There's no rush."

"Just take my damn virginity!"

His mouth slammed over hers, and she was thrilled at the victory. His hand delved between her legs, and she moaned, rocking against his hand. She tore her mouth from his. "Please, please," she chanted. She couldn't wait anymore. She had to get this done.

And then he was ripping off his clothes. His erection made her doubt for a moment because she was petite and that was definitely not. And then he was kissing her again, his hands stroking down her back to her bottom, rocking her against him. She was crazed by the tantalizingly close touch, and she kissed him with wild abandon, her hands seeking out what she needed, guiding him to her. He stilled her hand and dropped his forehead to hers. "Are you sure about this, Kate?"

"Yes! Hurry up!"

He threw a blanket over the sofa where he'd slept all summer and gestured to it. She hurried over, opened her legs, and waited. He grabbed a condom from a nearby duffel bag, rolled it on, and settled between her legs. Finally.

"Now!" she demanded.

And he listened. Slowly, oh so slowly, he pushed inside her, watching her. Her lips parted, and she closed her eyes, waiting for the good part. He stilled and kissed her gently.

"Hurry up," she told him, grabbing his ass and pulling hard, which surprisingly worked. He thrust all the way inside, and she cried out from the sharp pain.

"I was trying to go slow." He kissed her, distracting her from the fading pain, his tongue delving, making her melt. She ran her fingers through his soft hair, relaxing with his wonderful kisses. After a while, he lifted his head. "You doing okay?"

"When does it get good?" she asked.

He groaned. "Now." He started moving and it did get better, and though he did try with a lot of good pumping action and hot kisses, she didn't have an orgasm like she'd hoped. He did, moaning into her neck with it.

He stroked her hair, still inside her. "How was it for you?"

"I didn't have an orgasm."

"You were in such a hurry. I didn't have time."

She patted his shoulder. "Thank you, Ian. I really appreciate your gentle, but firm initiation. If you could just lift your weight off me, I'll be going."

He smiled against her mouth and kissed her again. "You need to spend the night. Your initiation isn't complete until you've done a little more. In the morning I'll make sure your virginity is completely gone."

"It is gone."

"Don't move." He pulled out, took care of the condom, and returned to the sofa, settling them on their sides so his front was curled around her back. Surprisingly, given their height differential, they fit together like nesting measuring spoons. He grabbed another blanket off the back of the sofa and covered them both. "I'll show you what I mean in the morning. You need more experience." He kissed along her neck, which tingled like crazy. "It'll be better the second time."

"Are you sure?"

"Positive."

"Like a full-tilt boogie orgasm?" She really, really wanted to know what that felt like. She only had regular kinds on her own.

"Exactly like that."

She believed him. And it was true that she really did need more experience. "Okay."

She woke the next morning to Ian kissing her neck. He was on top of her and she giggled as he nipped at her. And then they heard the bedroom door open and footsteps. His brother, Barry, must've woken up. Ian nuzzled into her neck on the other side, and she smacked his shoulder. She'd hoped if they stayed still, Barry might think it was just Ian under here. The blanket ripped away from their heads. Luckily Ian covered her nakedness with his body.

"Kate!" Barry exclaimed.

She pulled the blanket back over them. "Don't tell Amber."

"Ian," Barry growled.

"Go away, bro. Geez."

Barry left, and Ian went right back to kissing her. He kissed her for a long time, down her neck, across her collarbone, her breasts. She never knew her breasts were so sensitive and when he sucked one nipple hard, her hips came up of their own accord. It was like a direct line of throbbing pleasure to her groin somehow. After she was thoroughly worked up, moaning and grabbing at him, she thought they'd do it, but then he kissed his way down her body and settled between her legs, kissing her where no one had ever put their mouth before.

She jerked against him. "What are you doing?"

He lifted his head. "I'm helping you lose the rest of your virginity."

"Like that?"

"Shh, yes." And then his mouth was doing deliciously dirty things that sent shockwaves of sensation through her. She moaned loudly, unable to keep quiet at the incredible pleasure. Her nails dug into his shoulders as he lapped at her.

"Don't stop, don't stop, don't stop," she chanted. He kept going and it quickly got intense, the pressure building unbearably. She was going to die if she didn't get her release. She whimpered incoherently.

He lifted his head and said, "Come for me."

A thrill went through her at the raunchy talk even as she decided she couldn't possibly—her mind shut down again as his mouth worked magic, and she broke helplessly against him, the sensation radiating outward through her entire body. He kept going, wringing every last drop of pleasure out of her and didn't stop until she went limp. She'd barely recovered from that when he thrust inside her again. And though the second time they did it was more pleasant, she didn't have an orgasm. She was forced to conclude that sex was just okay with him. No full-tilt boogie. Except with the mouth thing. But that wasn't actual sex.

When they'd finished, Ian held her again, but she really had to go. She'd accomplished her mission and was now an experienced woman ready to take on the male population of MIT. A whole new world awaited her.

She stood and wrapped the robe around her. "See you," she said.

"Come over later," he said.

"Maybe. I have some studying to do."

He stood, crossed to her, and rested his hands lightly on her hips. "I want to see you again."

"Thank you, Ian. I don't want you to get the wrong message. I'm grateful to you, but I'm only twenty-one, and I'm about to leave for grad school. I can't be hydrogen."

"Just with one guy?"

"Yes." She knew he'd understand. "I need to stay open to other male possibilities."

"Sowing your wild oats?"

"In a manner of speaking, yes." She left, and he let her, but even though she'd been very clear and had thanked him, he hadn't been quite done with her. He became puppy-eyed, following her around until they both left for grad school. By that time, he'd gotten the message, and she'd thought, with a mixture of relief and a strange pang of longing, that was the end of her and Ian.

3

———

Present day...

Ian stepped back from Kate after the kiss he'd been looking forward to for months. "What do you mean you have a boyfriend?"

She took off her glasses and industriously cleaned them on the end of her dress, which gave him a glimpse of shapely thigh. He yanked the dress back down, and she scowled at him before sliding the glasses back in place. "I have a boyfriend. What don't you understand?"

"Why did you let me kiss you? I gave you fair warning."

She smashed her lips together. He knew she wouldn't lie. She was a stickler for accuracy. "My libido trounced my brain. I blame your cologne for the short circuit."

He rubbed the back of his neck. "Is it serious with this guy?"

She tilted her head. "I met Dr. Cooper two months ago at the emergency room. I burned my hand while trying to cook cherries jubilee. Don't ask. Dr. Cooper, I mean

Christopher, has crazy hours, so we've only managed to go on six dates." She looked thoughtful. "There's been no mention of the L word, so I'd have to say it's a relationship with potential for serious if we spent more time together."

He got to the most important point. "Did you sleep with him?"

"Yes."

That hit him where it counted. The honesty thing was a double-edged sword. He went to her desk and sat down, trying to decide what was the right thing to do here. They'd hooked up last May right after she graduated with her PhD. He'd thought the timing had finally been right. He'd gotten over his breakup with Morgan (after a three-year relationship); Kate was finally done with school. He knew that even though Kate saw grad school as her time to sow her wild oats, after her first semester she'd lost interest in men in favor of her studies. By then he was involved with Morgan. But he'd never forgotten Kate, how could he? They'd been thrown together over the years because of their married siblings. And if he was perfectly honest, although he'd loved Morgan and the sex had been good, the chemistry he had with Kate had never been topped. Hell, he'd wanted to be with her after their first hookup, but she'd been too young and not ready for more. Something he painfully came to accept because for the first time in his life he'd really wanted a relationship.

Being with Kate changed him.

He'd been a bit of a player back then, a love 'em and leave 'em kind of guy. He'd never spent time just talking, really getting to know a woman like he had the summer they'd first met. He'd been staying at his brother's apartment while on break from grad school; she'd been staying with her sister across the hall, newly graduated from college. They talked about everything from mathematical discoveries relevant to computer science to why someone would scream during sex, which she postulated quite reasonably should only be a pleasurable thing. She had a sharp analytical mind with a unique perspective that made him always want to know what she was thinking. She was, in short, fascinating.

And so determined to lose her virginity before starting grad school that fall. His brother had warned him not to touch Kate. Her sister had threatened to kick his ass if he touched. Hell, even Kate had first said she was saving herself for marriage, which he believed and respected. But then she shed her baggy T-shirts and frayed jeans in favor of skimpy tops and short skirts. She stopped wearing underwear and pranced around in practically see-through summer pajamas at night. And then she showed up one night in nothing but a robe, informed him she was no longer saving herself, and dropped the robe.

A guy could only take so much.

That night with Kate (and the next morning) had made something abundantly clear to him—the sex was great because it was with someone he deeply cared about. He'd slept with a good number of women and nothing had ever come close.

Sometimes he liked to think she'd been saving herself just for him.

Kate had been about to start the same grad school that he went to, MIT, which had made him think they might continue what they'd started that summer. But the timing hadn't been right. She wanted a chance to date other guys, having had no experience before him. He understood even though he'd hated the whole idea of her with other guys. After their recent graduation hookup last May, she'd informed him she didn't want to do the long-distance thing, so he'd tried once again to move on.

But he couldn't stop thinking about her. He finally got some time off work and had flown out here to convince her to give the long-distance thing a chance. Her fellowship was for two years, only a year and a half left at this point, and then they could be together. She could look for work on the East Coast. There were plenty of universities there. He hadn't counted on a boyfriend. Barry and Amber hadn't mentioned one. How serious could it be if Kate hadn't told her sister? He knew Kate told Amber about everything important in her life.

"Turn around so I can change," Kate said.

"I've already seen you naked," he reminded her.

"I don't want to tempt you," she said in her honest way.

He heaved a sigh and turned to face the opposite wall. There were no windows in her small office, so it was pretty private. He heard a rustle and then a loud, "Aahh." Which reminded him a little too much of the noises she made when they were naked. He quietly banged his head against the wall.

"Ian! You're going to lose brain cells that way. Knock it off!"

He stopped and rested his forehead against the cool wall. He had exactly one week in Chicago. He was flying home Christmas Eve to spend Christmas with his family, something that was especially important to his mother since his father died five years ago. Plus it was his niece Violet's second Christmas (Barry and Amber's daughter). She'd understand more what was going on this year. It was time to lay his cards on the table. Carefully, so as not to scare Kate off. She was uncomfortable with emotions, no wonder, considering the way her parents were so formal and distant, but he felt, with some care, he could get through that defense.

"I'm turning around," he said.

"Wait!"

He waited.

"Okay."

He turned and it took everything he had not to reach out and touch. Her hair had come out of its bun and cascaded over her shoulders in waves. She only looked like that in bed. She wore a baggy white sweater and faded jeans. She'd left her glasses on the desk, and he had a clear view of bright blue eyes no longer obscured by the huge lenses. Her skin was smooth and perfect, a cute upturned nose, high cheekbones, a full bottom lip. "Kate," he managed.

She blinked a few times, seemed to remember her glasses, and snagged them, sliding them back in place. Then she started shaking out her sweater and looking all over the floor. "I seem to have lost my hair band."

"Don't worry about it."

She kept looking. "My hair gets in the way when I'm working."

"Can you listen for a minute?"

She stilled. "What?"

"I don't have a consulting job in Chicago. I came here to see you."

Her mouth formed a perfect O of surprise.

"I wanted to ask you to give the long-distance thing a chance. I really like you." *The head-over-ass in love with you kind of like.*

She rubbed her forehead and finally said, "But...I'm dating Christopher now." She stood there for a moment, brow furrowed, deep in thought. "When do you leave?"

He winced. "Can't wait to get rid of me?"

"No! I'm sorry." She frowned. "That came out wrong. I

just wanted to know how much time we have to hang out as friends."

"I have a week. I'm flying home Christmas Eve."

"I'm also flying home Christmas Eve. Are you going to Barry and Amber's?"

"Wouldn't miss Violet's second Christmas."

"Then I guess I'll see you there too. I fly back the day after Christmas."

He'd known she wouldn't stay back home long. She found it difficult to leave her work, and he understood that single-minded focus and immersion in equations, he was the same way when deep in a computing project. Which was why he was here, hoping to catch the brief window of time when things slowed down before Christmas to convince her there was something between them worth pursuing. He'd seen her last Christmas too for Violet's first Christmas, but he'd brought a new girlfriend. Total rebound situation only three weeks after his breakup with Morgan. He'd picked Olivia up at Build-a-Bear after she helped him choose Violet's first teddy bear. He ended things with her the day after Christmas because one look at Kate enthusiastically explaining to their eight-month-old niece why the color violet always appeared at the bottom of the rainbow due to its shorter wavelength and greater refraction of light made him realize it was pointless. He would never want anyone the way he wanted Kate. An uncomfortable fact that had pricked his conscience whenever he'd seen Kate during the Morgan years. Dumping his rebound girlfriend made no difference in the Kate situation. She'd already headed back to work the day after Christmas, deep in postdoc applications.

"We could share a cab ride to the airport," she said. "My flight's nine a.m. into La Guardia. Same flight?"

"No, I'm seven thirty into JFK."

"We could still share a cab."

He crossed to her and caught her citrusy grapefruit scent, which he knew was from her shampoo because she'd asked him to sniff her hair and give his opinion when she'd first bought that kind four years ago. He didn't dare linger to breathe her in. That path only led to wanting to strip her down and taste her everywhere. "Maybe I should let you get back to work. Text me if you want to get together."

She brightened. "I will. I'm seeing Christopher tonight to exchange gifts, but I'm free tomorrow. How about dinner? As friends, I mean."

"Great," he muttered, brushing by her.

She put a gentle hand on his arm. "Ian, don't be mad. I didn't know you were coming here. I thought we were free to date other people." She looked down. "I'm not trying to hurt you. Please let's still be friends."

He had to force the words out. "We're friends. We'll hang out. I'm stuck here for the week anyway."

She dropped her hand and a pang of guilt made him try to smooth things over. It wasn't her fault he'd surprised her like this. Of the two of them, he'd had a girl-friend much more of the time than she'd had a boyfriend. "Have you seen Violet lately? She's getting so big." Violet was nearly two and so cute. Blond hair like her mom, brown eyes like her dad. Her hair would likely darken. He and his older brothers, Barry and Daniel, had all been blond when they were little.

She beamed, and his heart kicked up. Kate rarely smiled, too serious most of the time, but when she did, it was spectacular. "I Skype with her every Sunday. She's brilliant! You noticed it too, right?"

He found himself smiling. "How could I miss it?"

"She's only twenty-one months, but she already knows

all her colors, especially violet. She can count to twelve, and knows half her ABCs. Up to N. I'm working on getting her to P. She can also moo and do silly dances, thanks to Barry. Have you seen her cow bib and hat?"

Barry owned a fro-yo shop, The Dancing Cow, and loved to dress up like a cow to entertain the kids. Naturally, he dressed his daughter like a cow to join him.

He grinned. "I did."

Her blue eyes lit up behind her glasses. "I've been trying to think of the perfect Christmas gift for her for weeks. She's a little young for a tea set and not quite ready for an Emma doll. That's the kind that can really drink a bottle and get diaper changes. Like a real baby." She shook her head, murmuring, "I'll think of something."

He was surprised by Kate's girly gift ideas. He'd thought she'd get Violet a telescope or a model of the solar system. Though she had gotten Violet a cute plush mermaid rattle last Christmas now that he thought about it. He spied her hair band on the floor and handed it to her.

"Thanks." She put her hair back up in its usual messy bun and returned to her desk. "I'll text you tomorrow, okay?"

He wanted to say *don't sleep with Christopher tonight*, but he had no right. "Yup." He stopped in the doorway and watched her expression when he added, "Have a good time tonight."

She was already deep into whatever work she'd pulled up on her computer. He quietly shut the door behind him.

~

Kate carefully wrapped the large painting that was her gift for Christopher, stuck it in the roomy trunk of her blue

Subaru station wagon, chosen for its tremendous safety record, and drove over to his apartment building near the hospital where he worked. They'd be exchanging gifts tonight because he had to work the weekend shift at the hospital in order to get off for Christmas the following weekend. She loved this painting and almost kept it for herself, but she felt it important to give a thoughtful gift to your boyfriend with potential for more. Christopher was handsome, smart, successful, with a wonderful history of longevity in his family. He was, by any estimation, ideal husband material. He was a good kisser too. A seven in the bedroom, but that wasn't horrible. They'd slept together twice. The best thing was she never lost focus with him due to her libido, so she felt confident her work would always have priority in her brain-space.

She parked in the underground parking garage of his building and rode the elevator up to the lobby, where Christopher buzzed her in.

He answered the door with a big smile, which she returned with a small smile of her own for the sake of politeness. She wasn't in the habit of big smiles for no good reason. It reminded her of a chimpanzee baring its teeth, which was never a friendly sign. Christopher was nicely average—average height (five ten), average weight, and build. Short, dark brown hair, brown eyes, clean-shaven, typically. He smiled a lot like he found something funny, though she was often confused as to what exactly that was. "Merry Christmas, Kate."

"Merry Christmas," she said, though she couldn't help but think it wasn't yet Christmas so they should hold off on that greeting.

He inclined his head. "That's a huge present you've got there."

"Here." She shoved the large painting in his hands. She

dropped her purse and took off her wool coat, watching with increasing irritation as he carefully and slowly took off the paper. Everyone knew you were supposed to tear off the paper as quickly as possible. She used the minimal amount of tape so he could do exactly that.

Finally, the painting was revealed. An Amber Lewis-Furnukle original. It was a cow in a field of grass. One of Amber's rare figurative watercolors. Her sister was a very talented artist who'd sold paintings to galleries. Most of the paintings were abstracts. This painting was bound to be collectible due to its rarity.

Christopher laughed. "A cow? Wow." He shook his head. "That's nice. Thank you."

"It's not nice," she huffed. "It's a rare, original water-color by my sister, an up-and-coming artist. I'm sure it'll only increase in value due to its rarity. I thought you appreciated art." She gestured to the geometric paintings that hung on the walls of his living room.

He kissed her cheek. "I do. Thank you. I really like it. And I'm not surprised your sister's an artist. You always have a Bohemian look going on."

"I do?"

"Yeah, the rumpled hair, the long sweaters, the frayed jeans. It's cute."

"My hair's not rumpled. It's in a bun."

He touched her bun. "Kind of half in, half out. Bohemian."

She stiffened, slightly alarmed at how little he seemed to know her after six dates and two nights of okay sex. "I'm not Bohemian at all. I've been wearing the same clothes for the last seven years because they fit and they're comfortable. My hair's in a loose bun because I need it out of the way, but I don't want it distracting me with a tight pull away from my face."

"Okay, okay, you're not Bohemian. Here, let me get your gift." He crossed to the end table and picked up a small black velvet box. Her heart pounded like crazy. Was he going to propose? She should say no, right? She should say they needed more time to get to know each other. One of them needed to say the L word. Though she, personally, had never said it to anyone ever. Not even her family. Her family wasn't very expressive. Her parents were physicists, like her, and spent most of their time figuring out the wonders of the universe, not coddling their daughter, who happened to grow up in their universe. Her sister, Amber, was much more expressive. She had a different mother than Kate, though both of their mothers were blond and petite (her father had a type, apparently), which explained why they resembled each other a bit in looks, but not at all in personality traits.

He pressed the box into her hand and grinned. "Open it."

She girded her loins. Then she quickly opened it and stared at a gold charm bracelet with a bunch of beads and shiny doodads and in the center a miniature Christmas wreath studded with tiny diamonds. It was the same bracelet she'd seen advertised all over the city—on billboards, on bus stops, on the el. This was the bracelet thousands of women were wearing this Christmas. A gift that required no thought behind it whatsoever. Besides that, she didn't even wear jewelry. She didn't like anything on her body to distract her from the single-minded focus needed for work. This would ride up and down her arm all day long, irritating her, and she couldn't wear it in the lab at all.

She shut the lid with a snap. "Thank you for the gift."

"Put it on," he said, opening the lid again. He took it out and put it on her. "Beautiful."

She was about to undo the clasp when he tilted her face up and kissed her. A small tingle went through her. She kissed him back, hoping to lose the memory of Ian's kiss earlier, which she should probably tell Christopher about, considering honesty was very important in relationships. Were they in a relationship? She wasn't sure. They hadn't talked about it, actually, maybe they should—

He stopped kissing her.

"You okay?" he asked. "It feels like you're a million miles away."

Ridiculous. She was standing right in front of him. She got to the point. "A friend is in town. His name is Ian, and I'll be going to dinner with him tomorrow night. As friends." She nodded once. "I thought you should know."

He raised a brow. "Ex-boyfriend?"

"No, he was never my boyfriend. It was a purely physical relationship."

Both of his brows shot up. "Oh, yeah? Maybe I'll join you."

She froze. "I thought you had to work tomorrow."

"I do. Stop by the hospital at five. I get an hour break for dinner. We'll go someplace nearby."

She scrambled to come up with a good reason why he couldn't meet Ian. This meeting of men who'd slept with her could only be awkward at best, territorial male posturing at worst. "Why do you want to meet him?"

He took her hand. "Any friend of yours is a friend of mine."

Nerves raced through her. "I fail to see—"

"Just tell him I'll be there too."

She couldn't see any possible scenario where this would go well. But before she could figure out what to say, Christopher started gently kissing her neck. This foreplay always signaled a trip to the bedroom.

4

"Will you do that for me?" Christopher whispered in her ear. The proximity of his voice to her ear didn't have the same hot tingle effect as when Ian had made a similar move earlier and that gave her pause. More than a pause. Alarm bells were going off in her head.

"I doubt he'll want to go," she said.

"Let me know either way." Then he licked her ear, which was weird because she couldn't hear for a moment.

She backed away. "I need to go home and call my sister."

He gave her a small smile that indicated amusement, though nothing was funny. In fact, she was on the verge of full-out panic. "Why don't you just call her from here?"

"I need privacy." She turned, grabbed her coat and purse, and headed to the door. "I'll let you know about tomorrow."

"Gimme a call when you're done talking to your sister. I'll come over."

"Maybe," she said as she shoved her arms into the sleeves of her wool coat. The charm bracelet jabbed the underside of her arm as the sleeve caught on it. She bolted out the door and headed down the elevator to her car. She was severely disturbed by the night's events: 1) Christopher's kiss wasn't nearly as lusty as Ian's, 2) Christopher thought she was Bohemian when she was the furthest thing from that, and 3) the thoughtless gift he'd given her. She couldn't even wait to get home to call Amber. She called her from her parked station wagon.

"I have a problem," she blurted as soon as Amber answered.

"Kate?"

"Yes."

A beat passed in silence.

"Aren't you going to ask what my problem is?" Kate asked with some irritation.

"I heard Ian's in Chicago. Is he the problem? Hold on." Then she spoke in a sweet voice that she saved for little Violet. "Go with Daddy for tubby time. I'll be up for mermaids." Then in her normal voice, "Okay. It's Violet's bath time."

She heard Barry singing *yo-ho-ho* and Violet giggling. A pang of longing went through her. How much nicer it would be to have a friendly, happy home like Barry and Amber had instead of sitting in a cold station wagon fretting over a terrible predicament.

She almost envied Violet. Amber and Barry were raising her great, teaching her lots of stuff while also giving her plenty of playtime. Kate had never had playtime as a kid, though for a while she'd really tried to get it. Like that Emma doll she'd desperately wanted and already knew she'd get Violet when she was four. Maybe some dress-up princess clothes too. All the things Kate had wanted as a girl, but her parents had deemed a frivolous gender-constricting waste of time. Kate had been alone a lot as a kid. Amber had been a teenager when she moved in with them (after Amber's mom took off for Paris) and didn't want to hang out with her little sister Kate much back then. Kate had hoped the Emma doll would be her companion in her quiet, formal household, and she'd planned to take good care of her too with a regular feeding and diaper-changing schedule. She'd asked for Emma for every birthday and every Christmas from five years old (when she'd first seen the commercial) until the embarrassingly old age of twelve. Instead she'd gotten a lecture in feminism from her mother and a series of scientific instruments—telescope, Gauss meter, and oscilloscope to name a few. By thirteen she gave up on the doll and dedicated herself to her studies. Amber had moved on to college by then and started taking an interest in Kate, being nicer and hanging out with her more, so Kate had at least felt less lonely.

Kate heaved a sigh. "Did you know Ian would be in Chicago?"

"Just found out an hour ago when he called Bare."

"He wants to begin a long-distance relationship with me, but I have a boyfriend." She got sweaty just thinking about it. She'd thought what she had with Christopher was ideal, but tonight, fresh from being with Ian, she realized that things with Christopher weren't as perfect as she'd thought.

"How come you didn't tell me about your boyfriend?" Amber asked. "I just found out about that too."

"I don't know." She felt queasy saying that because she knew perfectly well why she hadn't mentioned him. She hadn't wanted Ian to find out and feel hurt after their most recent hookup. It was easier to be friends with Ian if they didn't bring up other sexual partners. She'd never felt comfortable around Ian's girlfriends. "I've only seen

Christopher a handful of times because of our schedules."

"So-oo-oo, tell me the problem," Amber said.

"Christopher was doing the kissing-the-neck thing." She touched her neck. "You know, foreplay. And I suddenly felt like I couldn't ride the wild thing. I bolted out of there like he was Satan. But he's not! He's a doctor and good husband material." Ever since Violet was born, Kate had been thinking more and more about finding a husband and having kids of her own.

"Uh-huh."

"It's not logical to turn him down given that Christopher lives here and Ian lives not here. Something's wrong with me."

Amber murmured noncommittally.

"I like to be logical," Kate went on. "Anything else is chaos. The universe naturally unfolds into chaos, I know that, but I just don't want my life to be like that. I want it to make sense." She began a frantic one-handed cleaning of her car, which was littered with half-empty bottled waters, crumpled tissues, and Post-its covered in equations she'd scribbled down at traffic lights.

"Ian changed after he was with you," Amber said. "I think…"

Her hand involuntarily flexed, crumpling the Post-its together. "What?"

"I think you had a big influence on him. He stopped being a player after that. Got a little more serious."

She tossed the crumpled paper in the backseat to be dealt with later. "That makes no sense. The deflowering changed me, not him." She'd never told her sister about her recent graduation hookup with Ian. She was too embarrassed to admit her terrible lack of control around him. She snatched a bottled water off the floor and pressed it to her forehead, trying to cool off from thoughts of Ian.

"Kate," Amber said gently, "he's in love with you."

Kate gasped and dropped the bottled water right on her foot. "Ah!"

"Are you okay?"

She snatched the water and tossed that in the backseat too. "He's not in love with me!" He'd never said he loved her. Not once.

"He is, sweetie. Has been for years."

Kate did a quick rewind through her conversation earlier with Ian. He'd clearly said he *liked* her. "He never said he loved me."

"How do you feel about him?"

She fidgeted, suddenly uncomfortable as she delved into the murky waters of emotion. "He's...I don't know. He's a good friend. He's always been good to me." Her throat got tight. "I don't know," she finished lamely.

"Uh-huh. And how do you feel about Christopher?"

"He's got husband material written all over him. Smart, successful, good genes."

"Do you love him?"

"Which one?"

"Either."

Her gut churned. "I don't know. How do you know?"

"Trust me, you'll know. Sweetie, I know our family is not big on love. And I don't know Christopher, but I do know Ian. And he's turned out great. He's also smart, successful, with good genes. And he really does love you. Just give him a chance. I think if you open your heart just a little, you might be pleasantly surprised."

"I don't like surprises." This was making her head hurt, and her stomach do another slow, painful churn. Nothing was clear in this area at all. Except one thing. Men were a major distraction. "Amber, do you know why I graduated high school in three years?"

"Because you studied a lot?"

"Because of Billy Hall. I had a huge crush on him my entire second year, and I lost all focus. I should've graduated in two years." That really burned. She would've been much further ahead in her research if she hadn't fallen a year behind back then. Her mom had drilled it into her after that spectacular failure that academics came first. And if Kate wanted a partner down the road, her mom told her a work partner was best, life partner second. That's the kind of marriage her parents had—both physicists at the same university.

"Wow, *two* years," Amber said.

Kate hurled a few more half-empty bottled waters in the backseat. "Same thing happened at MIT. My first year I lost focus because I was on the prowl for men."

Amber giggled.

"It's not funny. There really is a short circuit between my brain and my libido."

"But you're done with school. You can have a career and a boyfriend. Not everything is either-or, black or white. There's a lot of gray area."

She leaned down to the passenger-side floor and snagged some crumpled tissues, a napkin, and a half-eaten granola bar. "I don't like gray areas." She stuffed all the trash in the cup holder. "I like absolutes."

"Take my mom, for example. Do you think I want her to visit? No. But she wants a relationship with Violet. Am I going to deny my daughter the chance to get to know her grandmother? No. *Gray area.*"

Kate rested her forehead on the steering wheel. "I still don't know what to do," she whispered.

"You can have both. A guy and a career. It's a gray area

I'm encouraging you to explore. And, honestly, the fact that this wasn't a big issue for you with your current boyfriend and just thinking about it with Ian has got you worked up tells me that there's something worth exploring with Ian."

Kate's mind leaped to a major roadblock. "If things didn't work out with Ian, I'd lose him as a friend. And family get-togethers would be *so* awkward." Everything with Christopher seemed so much simpler. And, really, the simplest answer was often the most elegant. In physics, anyway. Why couldn't life be as clear-cut as science? Her thoughts ping-ponged all over the place so she couldn't even think clearly. She took a deep breath when she realized she'd been holding her breath. Amber interrupted her silent meltdown.

"Bare and I discussed it already—"

She shot straight up in her seat. "You did?"

"Well, yes, we knew how Ian felt about you. And we're on board. Bare will smooth things over if need be. You know how good he is at that." It was true. Barry got along with everyone, even Kate's mother, and always made sure everyone felt welcome and comfortable at his and Amber's house, where they all gathered for holidays.

Kate pulled her hair band out and redid her bun. "Ian's very distracting. When I first moved here…" She stopped herself. Ian had sent her some very suggestive texts when she'd first moved to Chicago (after their most recent hookup that her sister still didn't know about).

"What did he do?" Amber asked eagerly.

She blew out a breath. Who else was she going to tell? "He sexted me."

"Augh, don't tell me."

"Like, *I found Schrödinger's cat.*"

"I don't get it."

"He means my kitty! He's a dirty, raunchy talker. How am I supposed to focus when I'm getting texts like that? Oh, here's another classic Ian text, *optimum logarithm*."

"Explain," Amber said.

"It's a play on words. He means my rhythm, his log. Optimum, the best, together. You see the problem?"

Amber didn't reply at first. "Hold on," she gasped out.

"Amber, are you okay?"

"Woo! Yeah, sorry. Just thought about something funny Violet said today. So maybe you could set some boundaries with him. No texts or phone calls during work hours except in case of emergency. I'm sure Ian supports your career. We're all so proud of you. Maxine told us you're doing groundbreaking research."

That was her mom. Always bragging on Kate's scholarly accomplishments. She took full credit for pushing Kate to excel. "It's very exciting. Dr. Weintraub wants to apply for funding to keep me on an extra year so I can continue it."

"I thought you didn't want to stay postdoc too long. You wanted a tenure position."

"It's hard to turn down an opportunity like that if it came through. The facilities here are incredible." She could hear Barry hollering for Amber in the background.

"I gotta go, sweetie. The mermaids await. Love you! Call me if you need to talk some more."

Kate hung up and decided to call Ian, figuring she should get the whole meeting Christopher thing out of the way. She pulled down the visor and inspected her hair. What was she doing? It wasn't like Ian could see her through the phone. She slammed the visor back in place and dialed. "Christopher wants to join us for dinner tomorrow." Her breath came out in a cold puff. She should probably drive home soon, but there was just so much she had to clear up before she could leave the parking garage.

"Hi, Kate. Alright."

"Hi." She paused. "You actually want to go?"

"I'd love to meet him."

"Why?"

"I want to see who you get serious about."

"He gave me a bracelet with a diamond Christmas wreath."

"You don't wear jewelry."

She was simultaneously relieved that Ian knew her that well and dismayed that Christopher had never noticed her lack of jewelry. Of course she'd only known Christopher a couple of months. On the other hand, it had taken Ian less than two months to know her intimately. But Christopher had done nothing wrong, really. Most women would be thrilled with a gold charm bracelet. Just not her.

"It's the thought that counts," she said as much for his benefit as her own.

"I guess. What'd you get him?"

"Are you in love with me, Ian?"

Dead silence. Had she lost the connection? She pulled the phone away and looked at it. Nope. Still connected. "Ian?"

He cleared his throat. "Why would you say that?"

"Amber told me you were. Is it true?"

"We should have this conversation in person."

She really didn't want to wait. She needed clear-cut answers if she was going to make clear-cut decisions. "Why?"

"Because it's a personal conversation. Where are you? This is a strange conversation to have when you're with your boyfriend."

"I left during foreplay."

Ian made a weird choking sound. "Can I ask why?"

"I had to call my sister. I'd better go. I'm sitting in a parking garage and it's pretty cold in the car. I should head home."

"You want me to come over so we can have that personal conversation?"

"That would be good. It would help me clear up a few things. Or not." She pressed her fingers to her forehead. "I'm not sure. This must be the gray area Amber told me about."

"I love gray areas."

"Figures. This would point to a basic incompatibility between us."

"I think we're compatible enough. Give me the address."

She rattled off the address and hung up. Then she yanked up the sleeve of her coat and took off that irritating bracelet. She shoved it into the crumpled tissues in the cup holder and headed home for that personal conversation.

Ian drove over to Kate's apartment, wondering exactly what he was going to say. It must mean something that she'd left her boyfriend in the middle of foreplay—he'd about swallowed his tongue when she told him that—and was now willing to spend time with him. But did that mean she was dumping her boyfriend for him? If Ian finally told her he loved her, would she return that love or give him the cold shoulder? Things could go either way with Kate.

No wonder she was surprised by his visit. When they'd last seen each other seven months ago, he'd been angry at the way she rushed off after sleeping with him. Again.

He'd thought it had meant something to her too. He'd called her cold, and she really came off that way. But in the months since then, he thought of Kate with her parents, who he'd met on several occasions. Her parents were very formal and spoke stiffly. They didn't even hug Kate at her graduation dinner, didn't smile, didn't say any loving words. Merely formally congratulated her. He'd started to think maybe Kate didn't know how to show her love, but that didn't mean she didn't feel something. Because how could she let go with him the way she did in bed, when she was normally so in her head, if she felt nothing for him? He had no illusions that he was the world's best lover. It was only with Kate that the sex was that good. It was their natural chemistry together and, he liked to think, an intensity of feeling that went both ways. He really hoped so.

He rang the buzzer to a three-story brick building, and Kate answered the door a few minutes later. She stared at him for a long moment like she was seeing him in a whole new way and slowly blinked. Probably wondering about that whole in-love-with-you thing Amber had blabbed. He couldn't even fake a smile, merely returned her gaze as if to say *yes, it's all true.*

"Hi," she said before whirling away and leading the way up the stairs to her apartment. She looked exactly the same as when he'd seen her earlier—blond hair still in a messy bun, same baggy sweater and jeans, no makeup. Clearly she hadn't changed or made herself up for her date with the doctor. He and Kate had never had an actual date, so he didn't know if that was a good sign or not.

"How ya doing?" he asked.

She glanced over her shoulder. "Fine."

She opened the door and let him into an apartment that reminded him of an old dorm. Definitely university housing. Brown sofa, coffee table, small TV. Tile floors. The walls were plain white with no homey touches. Not even a single Christmas decoration.

"Why didn't you get an apartment off-campus?" he asked.

She lifted one shoulder. "They let postdocs stay in graduate housing, and it came furnished. Can't beat it for convenience and affordability. Drink?"

"Sure."

She went to a small galley kitchen separated from the living room by a half wall. The counter was littered with half-full bottled waters like she'd forgotten about one before picking up another. Post-its with scribbled equations were stuck on the wall over the sink. She started opening and closing cabinets, looking for who knew what, opening the refrigerator, then the freezer, back to the refrigerator before finally turning to face him. "I have water or milk."

She rarely remembered real-life stuff like groceries because she was preoccupied with figuring out the universe. He understood, he worked with computer science people thoroughly immersed in coding. He could be the same way at times, though he could turn it off and go back to real life a little easier than some of his colleagues. Probably his mom's influence, she was an affectionate woman who loved art and theater. He and his brothers took after their dad, a brilliant mechanical engineer, in their analytical bent, but tempered by their mom's insistence on pulling away from technology to experience the real world.

At least Kate, unlike his coworkers who often forgot to shower, was always fresh and clean because hot showers helped her have breakthroughs in thought. He wouldn't mind having a breakthrough shower moment with her. He adjusted himself discreetly. "Water," he croaked.

She cocked her head. "Are you okay?"

"Yes." He let out a breath and sat on the sofa. He was the one in her apartment, not Christopher, so that could only be a good sign.

"Ice?" she asked.

"Sure."

She poured two glasses of water from the faucet, apparently out of bottled water, grabbed an ice-cube tray and dropped some cubes into one glass. "Would you like a straw too?"

It wasn't like Kate to fuss over him. Though it was kinda nice. "Sure."

She put the ice-cube tray away and started opening and closing cabinets again, presumably looking for a straw.

"Never mind!" he called.

She nodded once, grabbed both glasses, and joined him on the sofa. "Should we have our personal conversation now?" She set both glasses on the coffee table and looked at him expectantly.

That was the thing about Kate. She never danced around a topic. Everything she said was honest, direct, and to the point. Something he usually appreciated, though this particular topic required easing into. He picked up his glass with ice, took a long drink, and set the glass on the coffee table next to her untouched glass. "Did you break up with Christopher?"

"No."

He shifted toward her. "Why did you leave in the middle of foreplay to call Amber?"

She bit her lip, and he waited, knowing she'd blurt out the truth if he was patient.

She folded her hands in her lap before saying quietly, "I'm uncomfortable confiding that to you."

He leaned closer. "Was it about me?"

She swallowed visibly. "Yes."

A surge of triumph went through him. "What did you say about me?"

She looked thoughtful and finally said, "I told her you were a distraction."

"Does Christopher distract you?"

"No."

Given enough questions, he thought he could get the whole conversation out of her, but what he really wanted to do was kiss her again. He leaned in, giving her plenty of time to protest, but she didn't. She met him halfway. He slid his hand into her hair and claimed her mouth. Things got hot and heavy fast. Their tongues tangled, her hands slid over his chest, and then he had her under him. It felt so good to press his full body against hers while he kissed her. She made these sexy little noises in the back of her throat that drove him insane with lust. He kissed and tasted her neck as he slid his hand under her sweater and pushed the cup of her bra out of the way so he could caress her beautiful breast.

"We shouldn't be doing this," she said weakly, arching into his hand. "I have a boyfriend."

"Ditch him." He kissed her again long and deep, the heat between them igniting again. Without breaking the kiss, he raised his body just enough to slip his hand down and unbutton her jeans. She shoved at his chest, and he lifted his head, breaking the kiss.

"Ian," she said in a breathy voice, "we should talk." Her blue eyes through the tortoiseshell glasses were dark and dilated. Her cheeks were flushed, her lips bright pink from his kisses. He didn't want to talk. He rocked his pelvis into her, and she closed her eyes, threw her head back, and moaned. It would be so damn easy. She wanted him. He wanted her. But something told him he shouldn't push her on this. He didn't want her having any doubts about them. Didn't want her thinking that what they did was wrong. He'd wait for her to dump Christopher.

He eased himself off her, and she scrambled to sit up.

He sat next to her, leaned his elbows on his knees, and let out a long, fortifying breath. "I'm in love with you, Kate."

He glanced back at her. She'd slapped a hand over her mouth. He wasn't sure why she seemed so surprised. She said Amber told her earlier, but maybe she needed more explanation. "Have been since the first time we hooked up. But you weren't ready for anything that serious back then. But this last time we hooked up, I wanted us to keep going, even if it's long distance for a while. I never forgot you, Kate." He swallowed hard. "Never really got over you. How do you feel about me?"

She was quiet.

He stared straight ahead. "Please say something."

"But you were with Morgan all those years. You loved her."

He nodded. "I did. But nothing has ever run as deep as what I feel for you. I think Morgan knew that on some level. She never liked you and I being friends. It's probably why she gave me an ultimatum, commit or move on. I had to move on because—" he swallowed over the lump in his throat "—you still had a hold of my heart."

She sucked in an audible breath. He glanced back; her blue eyes were wide. He pressed his lips tightly together and faced front again. It seemed everyone knew how he felt about Kate, except Kate. But now the truth was out, and it felt like his heart was just hanging out there in the wind, raw and exposed.

"Ian, this…I'm just hearing about this for the first time, and I'm trying to wrap my head around it. I had no idea you lo—" She coughed. "I like you. I've always liked you. A lot. Amber says you just know when you love someone, but I still don't know exactly how you know. I'm not so good with emotions. Amber usually helps me straighten things out, but I'm still…confused."

He turned to face her. Her blue eyes were shiny with unshed tears, her expression pained. He stroked her soft blond hair. "Hey, I know it's hard for you, and I normally wouldn't push you to do something you're not comfortable with, but this is different." He leaned closer, meeting her eyes. "I need you to do some soul-searching and really try to figure out how you feel about me." He leaned back. "And how you feel about that other guy."

"Christopher," she supplied oh so helpfully.

He stood, his chest aching. "So we'll all go out tomorrow. Then you decide. Me or him." He headed for the door because he couldn't take one more minute of being with her, yet not having her, not knowing she was his. Only his.

She leaped off the sofa. "Where are you going? Are you mad?"

He wasn't really. He just needed to know where he stood, and it was clear he wasn't going to get any answers tonight. She needed time to process his admission, time to think about who she wanted a future with. He stopped at the door and just looked at her. She wrung her hands together, her brow creased in a worried expression.

"I'm not mad." He shoved his unruly hair out of his eyes. "I, uh, well, we'll see tomorrow. And, after that…I guess we'll both know where we stand."

She wrung her hands together some more. "My brain

only works quickly with science. Once emotion is involved, it comes to a screeching halt. Please give me time to think this through. I don't—" Her voice choked. "I don't want to mess this up," she finished in a small voice.

He crossed back to her, pulled her wringing hands apart, and hugged her. She sank against him. He always felt like she craved being hugged, though she never initiated one. He'd only ever seen her hug her sister.

She squeezed him tightly, burying her head in his chest. "I don't want to lose you, Ian. You're so important to me."

His throat got tight. Now what was he supposed to say to that? They had a history. They were friends, they were lovers, they were connected through their siblings, they shared a niece. So many connections. But he needed more.

He untangled her arms from around his waist. "I'll see you tomorrow."

"Okay," she said softly.

It took everything he had to walk out that door.

5

Kate lay in bed that night, staring at the ceiling as she replayed her time with Christopher. Their dates had been nice. Dinners at upscale restaurants, action adventure movies they both enjoyed. He never pushed her to be anything other than what she was. Seemed to accept her hard-core focus on physics, the long hours she put in at the lab. He also put in long hours at the hospital, and she thought that was a plus in the compatibility department. He was an ideal boyfriend on paper, and she could find no real fault with him. He was attractive by any measure. She was sure a lot of women would want him.

She rolled to her side and thought of Ian. That was where things got murky and hard to figure out. She couldn't think of him objectively at all. He'd permanently imprinted himself on her body and soul by being her first when she was twenty-one. And then they'd stayed friends, kinda, well, not really friends. Friendly. His girlfriend, Morgan, didn't want them spending any time together as friends. She saw him with Morgan at numerous family get-togethers. And then Ian and Morgan broke up. Some part of her had hoped when she saw him last Christmas, a few weeks after his breakup, that maybe they could hang out again and recreate that closeness she'd felt the summer they first met. But he'd brought a girlfriend. Some tramp from Build-a-Bear. She'd felt foolish and retreated back to work the day after Christmas.

But then there he was again at her PhD graduation only five months later with no girlfriend in sight. Still, she hadn't expected to hook up with him that night. Not only was she leaving for her postdoc appointment in Chicago the next day (the research project was fully funded and the professor in charge wanted her there yesterday), but, in her experience after the three men she'd hooked up with her first semester of graduate school, a repeat hookup would be a waste of both of their time. If a guy didn't bring their best work in the bedroom the first time, it just wasn't going to happen. Having already been with Ian when she was twenty-one, she didn't see how sex at twenty-five would be any different. But he had a way of drawing her in, as easily at twenty-five as he had at twenty-one, making her libido trounce her brain. She wasn't proud of that. She considered it a terrible character flaw and a hazard to her career. As a woman, she had to work twice as hard to prove herself in the male-dominated field of physics.

So there she was, standing in her cap and gown, chatting with her parents before the ceremony about the particle accelerator she'd soon be working with during her postdoc and her planned experiments. Then she saw Barry and Amber arrive with Ian holding baby Violet and all coherent thought left her. She couldn't even respond to whatever her mother had just asked her. She hadn't known Ian would be there. He'd surprised her. She was terrible with surprises.

"What're you doing here, Ian?" she'd exclaimed.

He grinned. "I wanted to see you graduate. Congratulations! I heard you won an Algon medal. You must be so happy. Everything just like you wanted."

She knew exactly what he meant. She'd explained to him at Barry and Amber's wedding, shortly after grad school began, that she must dedicate herself to her studies. This was in response to him wanting to see her again. She'd sworn off men after her first two months at MIT had yielded five hookups (three guys) and a dangerous drop in grades from A to B-. She was a serious physicist and had to achieve while her mind was young and agile. And she'd done exactly that.

"I am happy." She kissed Violet's soft baby cheek. "Hello, Violet."

Violet smiled, revealing a full set of one-year-old baby teeth. "Tate," she said.

"Kate," she and Ian enunciated at the same time.

"Tate!" Violet hollered.

Kate and Ian grinned at each other. Violet was so cute.

Later, after the ceremony and a celebratory dinner with family, Ian asked her if she wanted to get a beer at a local bar to continue the celebration.

"Ian, you know beer makes me horny."

He grinned and shoved his wavy brown hair out of his eyes. "And I'm okay with that."

She giggled. He was so funny. "Okay."

One beer and she was in his lap. It was an easy move from there back to his apartment. He lived in Boston not far from where she went to school, but they'd both been so busy working that she hadn't seen him. Plus the girlfriend barrier kept them apart, except at a few family events.

Ian took her straight to the bedroom, and they slammed

together like no time had passed at all since their last kiss four years ago. The stress and tension of those four years of hard work at graduate school melted away as Ian took her out of herself. His mouth, hard and demanding on hers, made her knees weak, made her mind shut down. She melted against him as her long-dormant libido flared to life again. He pulled back, his brown eyes hot and burning into hers as he started unbuttoning her shirt. The pause in the action gave her enough time to think.

She pushed her glasses in place. "You know, I'm not sure a repeat performance is worth our time."

He pulled the band out of her hair and took off her glasses, setting them both on the nightstand. The world went blurry. Then he wrapped his arms around her, settled his hands on her ass, and pressed her against his hardness. "I'm sure it's worth our time."

"The first time we were together wasn't a full-tilt boogie. Remember?"

He groaned and ground against her, which made her temporarily lose her train of thought. Then he was kissing her neck and unbuttoning the rest of her shirt, which brought her mind back on track. The first time she'd urged him to hurry up and take her virginity. And he had. No orgasm. Then he'd coaxed her into spending the night, saying a second time was necessary to make sure her virginity was completely gone. Still no orgasm. Except for the mouth thing.

The memories of their first time faded as right now Ian was stroking her all over her skirt—front, sides, and back. Probably looking for the zipper and revving her up at the same time. She turned. "Zipper's in the back."

He unzipped her and worked the skirt down over her hips. Should she explain the reason for her hesitation?

Perhaps he'd have a reasonable argument to sway her one way or the other. The merits of such a discussion—

She realized with a start that she was completely naked, and Ian was staring at her hungrily. She took the opportunity to explain exactly why she thought this repeat performance could be a waste of time.

"Ian," she said just to get his attention. He seemed to be fixated on her breasts. "I never had an orgasm with you."

"Yes, you did. You came right against my mouth." His shirt went flying. "I felt every shudder."

She throbbed at the memory, but still felt she had to explain her point. "That doesn't count. There was no penis involved."

"It doesn't count?" He enunciated each word clearly before he dropped his jeans and boxers. His erection sprang free, which temporarily distracted her. And then he rolled on a condom, which she didn't even know he'd had. Of course, her vision was—

He pulled her flush against his body. The heat and hardness of him made her soften and rub herself shamelessly against him.

He cradled her face with one large hand. "This time it will be full-tilt boogie *with* penis. I promise."

She wasn't so sure, but then he kissed her again and his hands were all over her, and her brain short-circuited in favor of her libido. She went up on tiptoe so they'd fit better, and gasped as his hand cupped her between the legs. Suddenly she wanted nothing more than to have him inside her despite all her earlier reasoning. It was raw and primal, and she couldn't fight it. She moaned loudly, beyond speech as he stroked her and slid his fingers inside.

"Kate," he groaned. He pulled her with him onto the

bed, and they immediately slammed together like powerful magnets, arms and legs tangled as they kissed and kissed and kissed. Then Ian rolled her onto her stomach, wrapped an arm around her waist and lifted her up on all fours.

"I don't like this way," she said over her shoulder. "This is what guys do when they want to forget who they're screwing."

He spread her legs wider. "I could never forget you. You talk the whole time."

"I do not."

He pressed at her entrance. "Let me show you how it could work for you."

She sighed. "Fine—oh!" He'd thrust inside her. "If you insist. Now see, this isn't much—" His hand reached around and stroked her rapidly. "Ah! I-oh, oh, oh."

"This counts, Kate," he growled in her ear as he rocked into her with deep, hard thrusts. "This totally counts. Penis involved."

"Oh-oh-oh," she chanted. The pressure was unbearable. He was rocking her world. Literally. Rocking her hard, stroking her quick like strumming a guitar. "Ohgodohgodohgod," she chanted. His heat at her back, the feeling of being surrounded by him, made the intensity ratchet up. She lost the power of speech as the pleasure escalated, higher and higher, until her insides clenched on the edge of release.

"Tell me it counts," he demanded.

"Please," she gasped. She was so close.

"Tell me." He thrust deep and held her there, his wicked fingers firm at her most sensitive spot, but frustratingly still.

"It counts!" she cried. He moved again, thrusting hard and stroking, and she saw stars, rocking helplessly as he took her over the edge and kept going, gripping her by the hips as he pounded into her. It was wild and animal, and she spiraled again, her body clenching around him. She screamed before she shuddered with a release even harder than the first. She panted, overwhelmed as he kept thrusting, the pleasure still intense, and then he let go with a hoarse sound. She whimpered as he pumped into her, bringing electric shocks of sensation. He finally stilled and held her tight against him, both of them catching their breath.

"Wow," she finally said. Her brain wasn't quite working yet.

"Yeah." He stroked her hair and kissed her shoulder. Then he pulled out, and she sank to the mattress. He flopped down next to her and flung his arm over her back.

After several quiet moments, Ian broke the silence. "The timing finally worked out for us."

That was alarmingly inaccurate. She rolled over and propped up on one elbow. "What do you mean?"

"You proved yourself academically. Maybe now you're ready for…more."

"The timing couldn't be worse. I leave tomorrow for a postdoc in Chicago."

He turned on his side to face her. "Why didn't you say something before we hooked up? I thought you'd have some time before you have to go."

"It didn't come up." When would it have? She graduated, they had dinner, beer, and then sex. There was no time to talk about the fact that she was leaving tomorrow.

She swallowed, her throat suddenly tight. Maybe she'd been afraid to tell him. Today was the first time she'd seen him without a woman glued to his side, and she'd wanted to spend time with him. She'd missed him; the memories of their summer together all those years ago had warmed her during those long, lonely nights she'd spent studying. She didn't make friends easily, mostly she had academic acquaintances. But hanging out with Ian that summer had been so easy and so fun.

He pulled her close so her head was on his chest. "We could do the long-distance thing."

She lifted her head. "I don't think I'd be good at that." What if she lost herself in her new research position? Once she was immersed in physics, she forgot the real world. She'd only hurt him. "Let's just call this a fun time between friends."

"Kate, it was more than that."

She didn't know what to say. How could she explain that she lost herself when she was with him and that was dangerous? She couldn't both lose herself in her work and lose herself in him. One of those things would suffer. She still had to prove herself as a physicist.

She sat up and climbed out of bed. "I should go."

He jackknifed up and shoved his wavy brown hair out of his face. "Don't you feel anything for me?"

She folded her hands together tightly. "I think it's easier to say goodbye now."

"For you."

She looked around for her clothes and quickly dressed. "Yes, well."

"Are you ever going to open your heart to anyone?"

She already had. With him. Otherwise this wouldn't be so difficult. "Goodbye, Ian."

He slammed a fist on the mattress. "You're so damn cold. I'm moving on!"

Hot tears stung her eyes. She wasn't cold. She was just doing what she had to do.

She'd barely made it out the door before she cried. The first time she'd cried since he'd rejected her initial advance four years ago. Every high and low in her life these past four years was bookended by her time with him. Why did Ian get to her so much?

Unable to answer her own question even now, she finally drifted to a restless sleep. She was caught in a dream, scrambling to solve unsolvable integrals, her mind stuck in an obsessive loop. She woke sweaty and cranky. Her emotions were all over the place, which made it impossible to think clearly. She knew if she didn't choose Ian, he'd be out of her life forever. But what if she said yes to him, they both went back to work, and she forgot to call him back or return his texts? Or worse, what if he was all she thought about and she lost focus at work? She'd never have any breakthroughs in her research if she spent all her time texting and mooning over him. Everything with Christopher was so much more clear-cut. They both did their thing and saw each other when it was convenient. She was never distracted by him. Christopher fit neatly into her life. Why should she choose messy?

She took a long hot shower, dressed, and tried to work on her laptop. After a few hours, she went for a walk, hoping that would clear her mind. She took the path by Lake Michigan and drew comfort from one of her heroes Albert Einstein. He said, "Problems cannot be solved with the same way of thinking that has created them." She needed a new perspective. She needed a breakthrough question to find the answer to this seemingly unsolvable problem.

She headed to her favorite place in all of Chicago—the Museum of Science and Industry. There were a lot of great exhibits there that she'd seen many times. Science at this level gave her comfort, but not the thrill of discovery. Mostly she liked to watch the kids get excited about science. She went through the rotunda and soaked in the beauty of the Christmas Around the World display with a huge forty-five-foot Christmas tree in the center and, surrounding it, smaller Christmas trees decorated by different ethnic groups in the community. She headed up a floor to find the one treasure that was completely different from all the science exhibits. The one quiet place with dim lighting that gave her a peek into a magical world—the Fairy Castle.

It was nine square feet of glorious enchantment. It dated from 1935 and each room was perfect in miniature with tiny furniture, tiny books, and fairy-tale paintings, even Cinderella's slippers and carriage were here. Her parents only let her read original fairy tales for their morality lessons, not the happy "sanitized" versions, but she'd still gotten a lot of joy out of Cinderella. The girl in rags that nobody noticed, cleaning the ashes, only to transform one magical night.

She slowly walked around the castle, immersing herself in each room. The miniature perspective always calmed her, making her imagine this tiny world and maybe her world (and problems) was just a miniature in someone else's larger world. The chapel had floor-to-ceiling stained glass, the Great Hall had a spiral staircase, and the library had miniature books, more than a hundred, hand written. She imagined herself living in such sumptuous luxury, descending the grand staircase in the Great Hall, heading to her favorite spot, Cinderella's drawing room, sitting at the table with the miniature chessboard while someone played the piano. Only who would be her opponent? Who would accompany her with music? Was she looking for a partner or someone in the background enhancing her life with the occasional pretty song? She circled the castle for an hour, and though she felt calmer, she didn't have a good answer. So she left to have a private chat with her secret confidante Rosie.

She headed to the museum gift shop where there was a collection of souvenir T-shirts and stopped in front of the T-shirt with that strong capable-looking woman showing off her bicep, her expression saying she took no guff—Rosie the Riveter. Though Kate knew the woman was a fictional creation designed to inspire women to work in factories and help their country while the men were overseas fighting World War II, there was something about her expression that made her want to confide in her.

What should I do about Ian? she asked silently.

Rosie stared back at her with an expression of *what do you think? Go to dinner with both and make a decision.*

What if I can't decide? What if I lose Ian? What if I lose Christopher?

You don't need a man. Look at me. I'm doing just fine with our boys overseas.

Maybe that was the best solution. Swear off men. Life was much simpler that way. Had been for her last few years of grad school. But now that she was working, she'd begun to think more of the future. Of maybe getting married and having kids. If she could find the right person. But maybe she'd found him years ago and just hadn't known it. Ian was three years older than her. That put them in different places in their lives back then, but what if right now they were finally in the same place? Of course, Christopher was five years older and was probably in a similar place in his life.

Rosie continued to gaze with her no-nonsense expression that said *be firm, make a choice, and stand by it.*

Still not sure what to do, she pulled Rosie off the hanger, and for the first time in their silent talks over the past few months, she paid and stuffed her in her purse for moral support.

When she got home, Ian was waiting for her, sitting in front of her apartment door. She quickly took off her fleece hat and smoothed her hair.

"How'd you get in here?" she asked.

"One of your neighbors buzzed me in." He stood and stretched out his long legs in jeans. She really liked when he wore jeans. They showed off his tight ass.

She pushed her glasses in place. "I said we'd meet over by the hospital tonight."

"I got bored."

She considered that. "Okay. Come in. But we still have two hours to kill before dinner." She put her key in the door and felt a hot breath by her ear that inexplicably made her shiver.

"I can't imagine what we'll do, can you?" he asked.

Her mind immediately filled with memories of their times together. Ian behind her, his heat surrounding her. Ian on top of her, between her legs. She hugged Rosie closer to her and went inside.

Ian flopped down on the sofa and stretched out, hands resting behind his head. "What'd you do today?"

"I talked to a friend." She yawned behind her hand, the warmth of the apartment making her sleepy and reminding her she'd slept horribly last night.

"You look tired. Should we take a nap?"

She looked toward the bedroom. That sounded so good. But a nap with Ian? She turned back to tell him *no* and jumped. He was right next to her. She hadn't even heard him get off the sofa. He took her purse and hat and set them down. Then he started unbuttoning her wool coat with those agile fingers honed to firm perfection on the computer keyboard and equally talented on a woman.

Heat flooded her. Why did Ian taking off her winter coat feel like foreplay? He was barely touching her.

"Ian," she said as a protest, but it came out all breathy.

"Shh, sleepyhead." He took off the coat, turning her, and worked it off her shoulders and down her arms. Then he headed to the sofa, draping the coat over the side.

She pulled off her boots, set them by the door, and looked at him from a safe eight feet away.

His mouth curled into an adorable lopsided smile that she found hard to resist.

She held up a hand like a stop sign. "You know we won't nap if we go in there." She, sadly, had no control with him. And he could be quite convincing.

He lifted one shoulder up and down. "Whatever happens, happens."

"Ian!" She let out a frustrated breath. She really was tired and had hoped to rest before her double-man date so she'd have a clear mind that would guide her into making the right decision.

"Hey." He crossed to her side. "I promise to let you sleep if you let me hold you."

She searched his warm brown eyes for trickery.

He laughed. "Don't look so suspicious. Have I ever lied to you?"

"No."

"I promise not to kiss you until you dump Christopher."

Her shoulders slumped. She should really call Amber for help in figuring all this out. Ian was clearly not going to be any help at all.

"Walk or carry?" he asked.

"Huh?"

"Carry it is." And then he scooped her up and carried her into the bedroom. It felt so good to be cradled in those warm, strong arms that she didn't protest at all, merely snuggled in against his chest. "That's my girl," he murmured.

"Wake me in an hour," she said.

True to his word, he tucked her under the down comforter, set her glasses on the nightstand, and spooned her from behind, a position that for some reason she fit with him best. She snuggled into the warmth of his body. He didn't kiss her or stroke her, just held her as promised, one arm wrapped around her waist. She let out a sigh and zonked out.

She woke when Ian whispered in her ear, "Wake up, sleeping beauty."

Slowly she became aware of his fingers splayed under her baggy sweater on the bare skin of her stomach. "You said you'd only hold me."

"I am only holding you."

"Over my clothes," she mumbled. His hand left her stomach only to stroke her hair back from her face. Sleep pulled at her. She hadn't felt so druggingly warm and relaxed since arriving in Chicago. Her eyes drifted shut.

"Do you really want to meet this guy for dinner?" he asked in a husky whisper.

"Mmm...sleeping."

His lips grazed her earlobe, his hot breath dancing over her skin, arousing her. "Did you ever notice how well we fit together?"

She had thought about that quite a lot. "The torso-to-leg ratio should make it not work."

He bent his knees, which made her legs tuck higher and simultaneously made her extremely aware of his hardness pressing into her softness. A deep throbbing between her legs took all of her attention. "Ian," she said softly.

"We work," he said.

He wasn't moving, yet the electric charge of attraction flared. Her body went into full arousal mode, hot and wet, which she suspected he knew. She was such a slut around him. "We shouldn't do this."

"You never left *me* in the middle of foreplay." He pushed her to her back. "Now kiss me."

"I can't. I have a boyfriend."

He stroked her cheek and cupped her face with one large hand. "You kissed me before."

She couldn't sleep with him now and then go out to dinner with Christopher an hour later. That wasn't fair to anyone. "I told you it was your cologne."

He half covered her, leaning over her. "Breathe deep, baby. Same cologne."

She giggled. He pulled back and grinned at her. Then he kissed the end of her nose, which she figured was okay. "All right," he said. "Let's go."

6

———————

Kate headed for the waiting room of the busy ER and settled into a corner away from the TV with Ian to wait. Christopher had texted he'd be out in five minutes. Ian headed to the men's room. She was wearing her new Rosie T-shirt under her sweater so she'd have the strength and wisdom to make a good decision tonight. Ian returned a few minutes later, loping toward her with his long-legged stride just as Christopher appeared walking several steps behind him. Both men smiled at her and she stared at them, a study in contrasts. Ian with his relaxed demeanor, rumpled hair, and kind brown eyes. Christopher with his quick agile movements, perfect hair that didn't move, sharp eyes, but also capable of good humor. She stood abruptly. Ian reached her first.

"Hey, they have one of Amber's paintings here," he said.

"What? Where?"

"In the men's room."

"Hi, Kate," Christopher said, leaning down and giving

her a quick kiss. "Thanks for meeting me." Then he offered his hand to Ian. "Dr. Christopher Cooper."

Ian shook his hand. "Ian."

She normally would've corrected the introduction with the fact that Ian was also a doctor, though it was a doctorate in computer science, not medicine, but she was so disturbed by the idea of Amber's painting hanging in the men's room that she left both men behind and marched straight to the men's room.

"Hey, lady!" some strange man said at the sink. "This is the men's room."

She stopped and stared. There, hanging over the urinals, was the rare, highly collectible extraordinary watercolor painting she'd given Christopher just last night. Fortunately there were no men at the urinals to shoo away.

"Weirdo," the man said before leaving.

She lifted the painting off the wall and headed out the door, keeping it tucked carefully under her arm. She crossed back to the waiting room, where Christopher and Ian were looking at her expectantly.

She stopped in front of Christopher and said as calmly as possible, "You hung this thoughtful gift I gave you in the men's room?"

Ian took a step back.

"It wouldn't fit in my apartment," Christopher said with not even a hint of remorse.

"Lie! It would've fit perfectly over the back of the sofa. This is an Amber Lewis-Furnukle original!"

"Who the hell is that?" Christopher asked.

Ian made a tsking noise. Christopher turned to him. "Shut up."

Kate lost it. "Don't tell him to shut up! Amber Lewis-Furnukle is my sister. I told you my sister made this painting! You thought I wouldn't find out about it in the men's room. But I did! Obviously you have no clue about art or the importance of my gift."

"Don't you think you're overreacting a bit?" Christopher asked. "It's just a—"

"I'm officially breaking up with you," she said and felt only relief when the words tumbled out. He didn't get her at all.

"Why?" he asked as if she wasn't standing there holding the giant error of his ways under one arm.

"Why!" she shouted. "Do I really have to explain again? Because you hung my gift in the men's room! And you don't give me hot shivers! And you're only a seven!"

Ian chuckled, and she felt herself flush.

Christopher scowled. "This isn't about the painting at all." He jerked a thumb in Ian's direction. "It's about him."

She lifted her chin. "Goodbye, Christopher."

He shook his head. "Whatever. I have real work to do, and I don't have time for drama." He headed back inside the hospital, storming through the door that said no admittance.

"What drama?" she asked Ian. "I was perfectly justified in feeling angry about this painting."

Ian's warm brown eyes met hers, and for the first time, all worked up like she was, she truly felt the love coming from him. He stepped closer and gazed down at her. "You absolutely were."

Oh, God, she'd been so foolish. How could she not have known, really known all this time that Ian loved her? She was so in her head that she hadn't let herself feel. But now she was overwhelmed with emotion, her throat felt tight, and her eyes stung with unshed tears of something so powerful that she felt like a complete idiot to have missed it. She carefully set the painting against a chair.

He opened his arms to her.

"Ian," she choked out before throwing herself in his arms.

And then he was kissing her, and she didn't need Rosie to tell her she'd made the right choice.

Someone wolf-whistled and she pulled away, suddenly conscious of their audience. He scooped up the painting and tucked it under one arm, then snagged her hand, and they walked out the door.

"So now what?" Kate asked after they'd walked a block away from the busy hospital entrance.

"Now we get this painting safely back to your apartment and then we start officially being boyfriend and girlfriend."

Nerves gripped her, and she stopped walking. "Ian?"

He turned back to her. "What?"

"I'm not sure how the long-distance thing would work." She wrung her hands together. "I don't want to mess things up."

One corner of his mouth lifted. "You think we need a plan?"

She nearly sagged with relief. "Yes, a plan would be great."

"Hmm…let me think on that." He hailed a cab. "Come on." He carefully tucked the painting into the trunk of the cab, and they headed back to her place.

Ian slid his arm around her in the backseat. "I remember when Amber made that painting. I joked that she should put Barry's face on the cow."

Kate laughed. "You're so funny."

"Now it's back to its rightful owner."

"Yes."

He pushed a strand of hair back from her face. "So you know what I'm thinking?"

She frowned. "I'm terrible at guessing what people are thinking."

"I think we should go on a date to begin the boyfriend-girlfriend part."

"What should we do?"

"How about the Museum of Science and Industry?"

"That's my favorite place in Chicago!"

"No!" he exclaimed in mock surprise. "The largest science museum in the western hemisphere is something that interests you?"

She grinned. "You knew. Can we do that tomorrow?"

"Yup." He pulled her close, and she rested her head on his chest, where she fit perfectly. "Tonight I'm taking you back to my hotel room."

"That sounds good."

He leaned down and whispered in her ear, "And I'm not stopping until you get a ten."

He'd already given her a ten the last time they were together, but she kept that to herself because she wouldn't mind another ten. "You could try."

He tickled her ribs. She giggled. "I can try, huh?"

"Yes!" she said on a laugh and then he was kissing her again, and there was no place she'd rather be than the back of a stranger's cab, all wrapped up in his arms.

"I-an!" she screamed before another shuddering release rolled through her. She groaned as he finally lifted his head from between her legs. They were in a king-sized bed in his hotel room. Ian had wasted no time getting her naked and in bed. They hadn't even had dinner. He said he was only hungry for her.

"Yes?" he said with a devilish glint in his brown eyes.

"That wasn't what I meant by a ten! It's not quantity of orgasms. It's quality of experience!"

He moved up her body, pausing to kiss along the way, her stomach, over her ribs, her breasts, and finally up to her mouth. "It wasn't quantity? Are you sure?"

He nuzzled into her neck and played with her breast, strumming her nipple with his thumb. Unbelievably, shockwaves of sensation arced through her. He'd already made her come three times.

"Ten orgasms isn't humanly possible," she gasped out.

He raised his head and looked at her. "Let's test that hypothesis."

"It's not a valid assumption. I explained that after the second one."

"It's hard to hear when your thighs are covering my ears." He pinched her nipple, and she jolted, drenched with pleasure. "I'll be the researcher and you'll be my subject."

"Control group?" she couldn't help but ask.

"Those sevens in your past who you'll never want again."

His hand slid down her body and cupped her sex. She cried out. She was way too sensitive to be handled anymore.

He gave her a slow, sexy smile. "So what exactly is a ten?"

She shoved his hand away. "You have to stop touching me so I can explain."

"Go ahead." He grabbed a condom and rolled it on. Then he returned and settled between her legs, resting on his forearms over her, waiting for her explanation.

"Well, there are categories."

"Really? What categories?" He rocked against her gently, and she moaned. "Tell me."

"Please," she gasped out.

He stilled. "Okay, now tell me."

"Thickness, dexterity, reciprocity, and alpha-level dominance."

He pinned her wrists over her head in one quick move. "Got it." He took her in one hard thrust.

"Oh-oh-oh-oh," she chanted and just when she was feeling that familiar tightening that meant she was about to go off, he lifted her off him, turned her around and settled her back, bending his knee in a way that gave her more friction. Three strokes later, she screamed.

"That's four," he said.

She just lay there completely limp, straddling his leg. "I'm done."

His hand stroked down her back. "I'm not."

She moaned.

~

Ian slid his leg down, letting Kate slide, and then arranged her on all fours so he could take control again. They were turned by the foot of the bed now so at least he didn't have to worry about her head hitting the headboard. She groaned as he wrapped one arm around her waist. He barely had to do anything to get her off now, she was in a feverishly high state of arousal, soaked with it, and hot to the touch everywhere. He loved that he could make her this way. He'd never had the chance to spend this much time making her crazed. He slid deep, and they both moaned. Nothing was like being inside her, tight and clasping around him.

"Let's go for five," he growled in her ear.

She trembled at the words, which was amazing because he'd barely moved. But then he did, sliding his hand to stroke her, pumping into her. She started chanting, "Ohgodohgod." It was when she stopped making noises that he knew she was close. He needed his own release after watching her go off four times, so he just went for it, thrusting deep while he kept one hand on her hard nub, letting it rock under his fingers while she kept chanting, urging him on, and then she quieted and shuddered against him with a hoarse cry. "That's five," he growled before he let go. He gripped her hips and lost himself, pumping until he had nothing left.

A few moments later, he pulled out, and she collapsed on the bed. She didn't move for several moments. Not even a groan.

"Kate?"

Nothing.

He scooped her up and settled her at the other end of the bed, resting her head on the pillow. She was sound asleep. He'd wake her with number six later.

Kate knew Ian would make good on his promise and follow through with numbers six through ten, which he did the next morning. She'd discovered that once she'd reached a peak level of arousal, multiple orgasms came easily. This discovery was most welcome and ensured many tens in her future with him.

After she'd zonked out the night before, she'd woken a short while later to a dinner from room service that he'd ordered for them. Then they'd spent the night cuddled up in bed, she sitting between his legs, with his arms wrapped around her from behind while they watched TV and caught up on each other's lives. Ian pressed her for her plans after her postdoc, but she didn't know yet. She'd always hoped for a tenured position at a university where she could continue her research, but which university might have a position for her was still unknown. She'd also given some thought to a one-year fellowship at a research facility like the large Hadron collider in Geneva. It was really just too soon to know, and she told him so.

He'd shifted her in his arms to meet her eyes. "Just make sure you keep me in the loop for future plans. I want us to have a future together."

"I will," she promised.

He kissed her tenderly in response before tucking her back in his arms. But she felt jittery even saying that. It was so hard to know what the future would bring, and she hated the idea of breaking a promise or hurting him, even if it was unintentional.

Now they were walking to the Museum of Science and Industry for their first date. He stopped and kissed her right in front of the museum. She wasn't used to the sudden intimacy in public and felt her cheeks heat. He adjusted her fleece hat around her ears, and that simple casual gesture of caring filled her heart with joy. He continued walking, and she sighed a swoony sigh of happiness.

Ian had never been to the museum before, and she showed him all of her favorite exhibits. She almost skipped the Fairy Castle, figuring a guy wouldn't be interested in it. He pointed it out on the map. "Hey, we missed this one."

She flushed. Sometimes she thought of the exhibit as just for her.

He smiled. "You like it, don't you?"

"It's a work of art."

"Well, let's go see it."

Ian laced his fingers with hers, and they walked over.

She pointed out every cool thing about the castle. He was especially impressed that water could actually spurt out of the dolphin's mouths in the tub in the princess's bathroom. It was amazing when you thought of the craftsmanship in miniature. Many of the pieces were historic, dating back hundreds of years, like the tiny amber vases from the Dowager Empress of China, and some ancient pieces in the grand hall, like a twenty-five-hundred-year-old Roman bust. She told him everything she knew about every piece.

"Which part is your favorite?" Ian asked, gazing down at her. A lock of wavy brown hair fell over his eye.

She pushed his hair back. "All of it."

"The Great Hall?"

"Yes."

"The chess table?"

"Yes. And Cinderella's coach in the magic garden and her glass slippers in the Great Hall."

He slid an arm around her. "You're a secret romantic, aren't you?"

Her cheeks heated. "I'm too practical for that."

"You should wear a beautiful gown one day like Cinderella."

She snorted. "I don't know when I'd wear that."

"We might find an occasion," he said with a mysterious tone.

She didn't know what he meant and didn't even try to guess. "Like what?"

"We'll see," he said.

"I don't do surprises well."

"I noticed," he said wryly.

After that, they went Christmas shopping for Violet in the museum store. Ian got Violet sand that retained its shape. Kate got her glow-in-the-dark constellation stickers for her bedroom ceiling. She'd make sure they were arranged for the summer sky, figuring Violet would spend more time outdoors looking at the sky in the summer. She spent a long time debating over a kids' T-shirt that said "Chicago" or one that said "Talk nerdy to me" while Ian looked around the store. She ultimately decided on the Chicago shirt, deciding that applying the label "nerdy" to a child could have a detrimental effect. On the way to the register she passed a collection of bins with kid stuff. She picked a pink frilly barrette with a little frog in the center out of one bin and continued to the register. She placed the items on the counter, then did an about-face and picked up a second barrette so she and Violet could match. She'd never had pink anything and definitely nothing frilly. She smiled to herself as she paid for everything.

She met Ian at the front of the store. He took her bag to carry it for her. "Let's grab some dinner and then we'll check out the Christmas light display at the Lincoln Park Zoo."

"That sounds good." She liked the holiday season, but hadn't had time to do any decorating on her own.

Dinner with Ian was so relaxed and fun—he always made her laugh and he was such a good listener—that Kate started to really believe they could do this long-distance thing. If they stacked up enough memories together, maybe it wouldn't be too hard to have long separations. She'd feared the longing between visits would consume her thoughts, but maybe she'd just be content.

When they got to the zoo, they were one of the few couples there. It was almost all families.

"You ever think about having kids?" Ian asked.

"Yes. Especially since Violet was born."

He squeezed her hand. "How many you want?"

"Two. I wouldn't want the kids to outnumber us."

His gaze was warm, his tone husky. "Us?"

She shook her head. She hadn't meant to jump ahead like that. This was their very first date, after all. "I mean, the adults. Look." She pointed. "The gazebo looks so pretty all lit up. I wonder if they have to add extra amperage to sustain this entire display."

Ian tipped her head back toward him. "I like dating you."

She turned to face him. "I like dating you too. Of course, it's only been one date. Then we have five more days." Her shoulders sagged. "It's not enough time. We'll be with family for Christmas, and then I'll fly back. I like this time just the two of us."

His hand cupped her jaw. "We'll have more time after this."

"When?"

"We'll work around your breaks and my vacation time."

"See, this is what I mean. I really think we need some kind of plan to set expectations. I don't want—"

Her worries halted when he kissed her. She fell into the delicious dizzy feeling, leaning up on tiptoe to get more. He pulled back and then gave her one more quick kiss.

"Ian," she admonished, "you short-circuited my brain again."

He grinned. "That was the idea."

She wrung her gloved hands together. "I'm worried I'll hurt you. What if I get my head lost in equations and forget to text you back?"

He put his hands over hers. "Would it make you feel better if we had a schedule?"

Relief coursed through her. "Yes."

He turned her back to the gazebo light display and wrapped his arms around her from behind so they could look at the lights together. "How about phone sex every Friday?" he asked in a husky voice right in her ear.

She stiffened, both intrigued and shocked. "I'm not sure I could do that over the phone."

"I'm sure you could." He nipped her neck and a jolt of electric sensation ran through her. "Can we accept that premise?"

She got serious. "I need your heat and hardness pressed against me, your—" He groaned. "What?"

"You'll be fine."

"Just from words?"

"We'll add in some visuals if the words aren't enough. Maybe I'll give you some instructions that'll leave us both satisfied."

"Instructions," she echoed.

He chuckled. "Yeah."

Ian had always come through in clear, understandable explanations when required. "Okay."

"Sunday night Skype for a regular conversation."

"That's perfect because I Skype with Violet every Sunday night."

"Yeah. Skype me after her privately."

"Okay." She turned in his arms. "What about during the week?"

"What's your schedule like?"

"I work every day until I can't keep my eyes open."

"What time is that?"

"Usually around nine or ten. Sometimes midnight."

"Seriously?"

She nodded. "That's often when the breakthroughs happen. When everything's quiet, and I have absolute focus."

"All right. How about you text me once your eyes get droopy?"

"What if you text and I'm busy?"

He kissed her quick and tapped her nose. "Then text me back when you're not busy."

"And you won't get mad?"

He gave her his adorable lopsided smile. "Nope."

"You can't text me dirty things," she warned. "Because then I can't focus."

He grabbed her by the hips and pulled her close. "Awww…you're taking all the fun out of it."

It wasn't the first time someone had accused her of not being fun, and she really did want to be fun for him. "I just…there's a short circuit."

He kissed her in a sensitive spot just below her ear that sent hot tingles down her neck. "From your brain to your libido, I heard about that."

"And you trip it all the time!"

He grabbed her and swung her around. "I love you, Kate." He set her down, and she put a hand to her mouth. He pulled her hand away and held it. "Why do you act so surprised when I say that?"

"I don't know. I'm just not used to hearing those words."

He looked at her with concern. "Didn't your parents ever say it to you?"

"No." He stroked her cheek, and she feared he was beginning to pity her. "Don't feel sorry for me! The underlying assumption was that my parents loved me. They wouldn't have taken such good care of me if they didn't. Boundaries and rules were spelled out. I thrived in that environment." She met his kind brown eyes and saw a tenderness looking back at her that she'd never seen from her parents. Her throat clogged with emotion as she realized that the environment she grew up in maybe wasn't as normal as she'd thought. "I can't say the L word like a normal person!" she cried.

Ian pulled her close, and she sagged against him. "Hey, it's okay," he said. "And I'm sure your assumption about your parents is right. Amber told you she loves you, right?"

"Yes," she said over the lump in her throat. She was beginning to feel like something was seriously wrong with her. She wished she could express herself as easily as Ian and Amber.

"Do you ever say it back to Amber?" Ian asked.

She lifted her head. "I try, but the words get stuck, and then she hugs me."

"You feel things, though," he said, "deep down."

She was so glad he was good at guessing because she was not good at explaining. "I feel so much, but it just doesn't come out the way it does for other people."

He cupped her head, holding her against his chest. "You're unique. That's why I love you."

She squeezed him even tighter, hoping he guessed from the extra squeeze how much he meant to her because the words were forever caught in her throat.

7

———

The days flew by as she and Ian went on dates every night after work, and he met her for lunch at work. The lab was closed the week between Christmas and New Year (though she'd planned to do some work from home), and she wanted to finish up a few loose ends before Christmas. Ian was a major distraction, but the lab was nearly empty as people left for the holidays, which made it easier to focus. Every day after a shared lunch in her office, Ian turned out the lights and gave her a pick-me-up. The first time, she hadn't known what he'd meant. He'd told her she looked tired and turned out the lights.

She'd laughed. "You expect me to nap here?"

"I'm going to give you a little pick-me-up." She felt the heat of him, close now, and his voice rumbled in her ear. "A little energy jolt."

He turned her and wrapped his arms around her from behind, kissing and nipping her neck.

"I do get a jolt when you bite me like that," she told him.

"Oh, yeah?" His teeth clamped down on the cord of her neck as he unbuttoned her jeans.

She found herself out of breath. "Ian." They couldn't do this here.

"Don't scream," he crooned in her ear.

She went damp, remembering all the times he'd made her scream back at his hotel room. She squirmed, but he had her tight, one arm wrapped around her waist. "I can't keep quiet when you—" The zipper of her jeans rasped down. "Oh, God," she said.

He pulled the jeans down along with her panties, and she knew she should protest. There were still some physicists wandering around the hallways. "There's people..." Her voice trailed off as his hand slid unerringly to her center, and her brain shut down.

"Ah," he said, his breath hot in her ear. "I love this short circuit of yours."

She stiffened at the way he sounded gloating, but his fingers gave her a pinch, shooting fiery pleasure through her limbs, making her cry out and soften. He turned her, pressing her against the wall, and covered her mouth with his, muffling her cries as he brought her to climax in a feverish rush.

And while she collapsed against the wall, panting and surprisingly full of energy, he turned on the light. She closed her eyes against the glare and felt him slide her panties and jeans back on.

"You like your pick-me-up?" he asked as he redid the zipper and button on the jeans.

She beamed. "That really worked! What am I going to do when you're not here to do that every afternoon?"

He cupped her jaw and kissed her. "Then you can think of me. Maybe I'll get you a vibrator for work. You can call it Ian."

She couldn't help but smile. She couldn't remember ever smiling as much as she did around him. "You're crazy."

"For you."

"Me too."

He grinned. "Stop by my hotel when your eyes are droopy."

Then he left, and she got back to work with renewed enthusiasm and energy with the knowledge that a well-timed distraction could actually add value to her research.

Kate stared eagerly at her gifts from Ian the day before Christmas Eve. They were sitting on the living room sofa at her place because Ian had checked out of the hotel. Her apartment felt very cozy and Christmassy now. Ian had decorated it while she was at work, stringing white lights along the ceiling of the living room and adding a small tabletop tree to the coffee table.

"Open yours first!" She gestured to the large gift box on the coffee table. She couldn't wait for him to open it. She just knew Ian would appreciate a thoughtful gift.

He snagged the box and tore the paper off in no time flat. "It's hand sanitizer."

"In the size approved for security checkpoints," she pointed out.

"Ah." He pulled out the next thing. "And a neck pillow."

"For sleeping on planes."

He pulled out a thin metal square. "And a small square." He held it up in question.

"It has a tracker inside it that synchs to an app, so you

don't leave any luggage or your laptop behind. I thought—"

He kissed her. "I love it." His warm brown eyes gazed into hers. "A very thoughtful gift. You wanted to make sure flying to see you was as safe and comfortable as possible."

"Yes!" She loved the way he really understood her. "Oh, Ian. I'm not ready for our time to end. This is the first time we've been boyfriend-girlfriend, and we leave tomorrow."

"I'll see you on Christmas at Barry and Amber's."

"I know, but then I'm heading back to Chicago. Besides, we'll be surrounded by our families."

He slid a warm hand to the back of her neck and squeezed, which for some reason turned her on. "I'm sure we can sneak away for a little while. Besides…the weather's looking dicey. They're saying a blizzard's coming. We could get stuck here and have our own Christmas."

"I've never had Christmas without my family."

"We'll be our own little family."

"Eww. We are not related."

One corner of his mouth lifted. "Our own cozy unit. Maybe." He put his gifts in a neat pile on the coffee table. "We'll see."

She couldn't help but pout. Ian leaned close and nipped her pouting bottom lip. A hot shiver ran through her.

"Let me guess," he said, "you don't like the uncertainty of the Christmas situation."

She really did prefer absolutes, even though life rarely gave them to her. "It's like you can read my mind. How do you do that?"

He chuckled.

"No, seriously, how do you do that?"

He handed her a gift box wrapped in shiny red paper. It was a perfect cube. "I know you, that's all. And you can be certain of one thing."

She smiled. "What?"

"I'll get you naked on Christmas either way."

"You're such a dirty talker." She kissed him and nipped his bottom lip like he always did to her.

He kissed her long and deep. "You're such a sexy woman. Now open your gifts."

She ripped off the paper, opened it up, and pulled out a coffee mug. It was Rosie the Riveter and it read We Can Do It.

"I love it!" she exclaimed.

"It matches your T-shirt, and this way you can be reminded whenever you drink coffee—"

"Which is practically all day!"

He rested one large hand on her upper thigh. "That we can do it."

She paused. "Do you mean we can do the long-distance thing or we can do, you know, it."

He wrapped a hand around the back of her neck and pulled her close, kissing her gently. "Both." He handed her a pink and white striped gift bag.

She flung the tissue paper off the top and pulled out a cute pink dress with spaghetti straps, a low-cut neckline with bits of lace, and a ruffled hem with more lace trim that would end mid-thigh. "Ian, this is so pretty."

"Try it on," he urged.

She could hardly wait. It was the prettiest most feminine dress she'd ever owned. She set her glasses on the coffee table, stood, quickly stripped down, and dropped the dress over her head. It felt like a cloud.

"Take off the bra," he said in a low voice.

She did, dropping it on her pile of clothes. She did a

little twirl, watching the ruffle poof out a little bit. "I can't wait for an occasion to wear it! Thank you!"

"This is just for us," he said, sliding his hand under the ruffled hem and lifting it to show her. She could clearly see his hand through the fabric. She hadn't realized how sheer it was until he did that. "It's not really a dress. It's lingerie. The saleslady called it a babydoll." He looked her up and down. "So pretty. I love you in this."

She sat next to him and played with the lacy trim on the end of the babydoll. "I never had anything pink as a kid and definitely nothing this lacy and ruffly."

"Why not?" he asked, pulling out her hair band and running his fingers through her hair.

"My mother didn't want me to be defined by gender stereotypes. She wanted me to feel I could do anything a man could do, including excelling as a physicist."

"I hope I don't sound like a complete sexist pig, but I really like you in dresses."

"Me too. As long as I don't have to wear pantyhose."

He stroked her leg. "Bare is definitely the way to go. And no offense, but I think your mom went too far the other way. I mean if you like being girly sometimes, she should've let you."

"I always felt like I missed out," she confessed. "My whole life was science. Every time I asked for a toy or a doll, I got a scientific instrument. Ian, I got an oscilloscope for Christmas instead of an Emma doll that can really drink and pee."

He laughed. "That sounds horrible. What's an oscilloscope again?"

"It measures voltages, particularly handy when troubleshooting a newly designed circuit." She cocked her head. "Which one sounds horrible? The oscilloscope or the doll?"

"Both. Why did you want a doll that can pee?"

She lifted one shoulder up and down. "She just seemed alive."

He stroked her cheek. "You wanted a sibling. A younger sister."

She nodded. "Amber's seven years older, and she didn't like hanging out with me until I was older. It was kind of lonely at my house. Kinda quiet. Not much fun for a kid."

"So you turned to books and science."

"That was the only option for me," she said. At his sympathetic look, she added, "But it wasn't that bad, really, we had a lot of interesting discussions about science at the dinner table."

He wrapped his arms around her and hugged her.

Tears threatened, and she blinked them back. "Science was a type of love," she said, though she was starting to realize it was a very limited type of love.

"I'm going to give you the whole deal," he said. "Not a type. The kind of love where you don't know where you start and I begin."

"You mean sex."

He stood and pulled her up with him. Then he pulled her arms around his waist and wrapped his arms around her. "I mean like a circle where you don't know the end or the beginning. Within this circle—" he paused and met her eyes "—represented by our arms around each other, is you and me. And it's filled with unconditional love."

Her heart squeezed painfully as she felt what he was offering at the same time as she understood what she'd been lacking. She nodded, unable to speak over the lump in her throat.

Without warning, he scooped her up and carried her to bed. And then he took her, with great care and tenderness that showed his love in every touch, every look, until there was nothing in the universe but him.

～

Ian carefully snuck out of bed Christmas Eve morning and checked his cell. Yes! The airport was shut down. The snow had been coming down hard last night, winds high, and they'd been warned it was a possibility. All flights were cancelled, giving him more time with Kate. He emailed the office, requesting the days off between Christmas and New Year's. It was nearly all his vacation time, but it was worth it. Then he emailed his mom to let her know he'd be staying in Chicago for Christmas, but he'd call. This was the best Christmas gift of all. He carefully shut off the alarm clock and slid back into bed, settling Kate against his side. She threw an arm and leg over him. He loved that she was so used to sleeping with him now that she just kept right on sleeping. This was their first Christmas together just the two of them. They'd already given each other their gifts last night, but that didn't mean they couldn't make it fun.

She woke with a start a short while later. "What time is it? I didn't hear the alarm."

"I shut it off. The airport closed. We're stuck here." He kissed her.

"Really?" She slowly blinked as she relaxed again. "Wow. The blizzard must be bad."

"Yeah, and the wind and the ice." He pulled her on top of him, and she rested her cheek over his heart. She often said she liked to listen to his heartbeat. "Our first Christmas together."

"I saw you last Christmas."

"I mean just the two of us."

She stroked his chest. "I want to cook. We'll make a holiday dinner just like back home. Turkey, mashed potatoes, green beans, Christmas pie."

"You know how to make all those things?" She didn't cook as far as he knew.

She lifted her head, her blue eyes sleepy again and unfocused. "I'll look it up online. How hard could it be?"

He played with a lock of her blond hair. He loved that he was the only one who ever saw her hair like this out of its bun, loose and flowing in beautiful waves over her shoulders. "You think we can make it out to get food in this blizzard?"

She slid off him and crossed to the window, peeking between the slats of the blinds at the white wall of snow. His cock pulsed just looking at her standing there naked. He snagged a condom from the nightstand and rolled it on. "Get over here," he ordered.

She turned with a smile and immediately climbed on top of him, taking him in. She knew that tone meant business. He gripped her hips and ground her down hard on him. She threw her head back and moaned. He kept moving her up and down the length of him, and she lifted her hair and shook it out nice and loose.

"Yes," he said, "I love your hair like that."

She moved on her own then, faster and faster, until he felt like he was going to explode.

"Come with me," he urged, sitting up and angling her so he could stroke her in just the right spot on the inside.

She cried out and went wild, whimpering and bucking. He kept a firm grip on her hips, making her take more, urging her on. "More, yes, more," he told her over and over until she broke with a long shuddering release that triggered his own. He exploded with a hoarse cry, holding her tight as the last tremors went through him.

He lay back and she went with him, lying on top of him, both of them breathing hard.

"Your heart is pounding," she said.

He couldn't speak.

She sat up, still straddling him, and put a hand over her own heart. "So's mine." She put his hand over her heart. "Feel it?"

"Yes." He yanked her back down on top of him and wrapped both arms around her in a tight embrace. She let out a sigh and relaxed against him. This was all he needed in this world. A naked Kate pressed against him. He didn't care how hard it was going to be doing this long-distance thing. If he could have this in the end, it was all worth it.

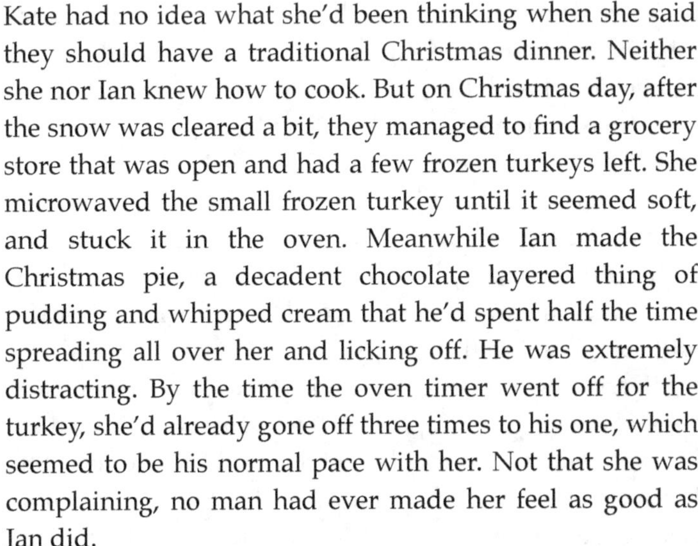

Kate had no idea what she'd been thinking when she said they should have a traditional Christmas dinner. Neither she nor Ian knew how to cook. But on Christmas day, after the snow was cleared a bit, they managed to find a grocery store that was open and had a few frozen turkeys left. She microwaved the small frozen turkey until it seemed soft, and stuck it in the oven. Meanwhile Ian made the Christmas pie, a decadent chocolate layered thing of pudding and whipped cream that he'd spent half the time spreading all over her and licking off. He was extremely distracting. By the time the oven timer went off for the turkey, she'd already gone off three times to his one, which seemed to be his normal pace with her. Not that she was complaining, no man had ever made her feel as good as Ian did.

Finally, she took the turkey out of the oven and let it rest before carving as the recipe said. Then she stuck the green beans in the microwave. While they cooked, she smashed the potatoes she'd microwaved earlier with a large fork and a lot of muscle power. Ian finished the job for her because the potatoes weren't looking very mashed.

Ian peered at the turkey. "Are you sure it's done?"

"Yeah, it's golden brown just like the picture."

"You think it's cooked all the way through?"

"I don't have a meat thermometer. Just wiggle the drumstick. That's what my mom does."

He wiggled it. "What's that mean?"

"I don't know. My dad always carves it after she wiggles it."

He shrugged and carved the turkey. "It's kinda pink on this one part." He pointed.

"So we'll skip that part."

He cut off the drumsticks and set them on a plate; then he added some white pieces of meat.

They sat on the sofa with the feast laid out on the coffee table before them. She turned on the TV to the Christmas carol channel with the image of a fireplace. Now it felt like Christmas at home, minus her parents. And Barry, Amber, and Violet. Gosh, she missed Violet. Still, it was festive. And at least she didn't have her mom snapping at her dad all day to help her in the kitchen, even when she always ended up criticizing his efforts and taking over anyway. She found she didn't miss the exchange of gift certificates with her parents either.

Everything was better with Ian, who was always touching her and kissing her, except when they were eating. Even then, his eyes always looked at her with a heated tenderness. She knew she was lucky to have him in her life. She looked at him, staring at the plate of food on his lap, and struggled to find the words to tell him how she felt. "Thank you."

He raised a brow. "For what?"

"For coming to visit me." She tucked a lock of hair behind her ear that had fallen out of her bun. "And for sticking around long enough to make the boyfriend part happen."

"My pleasure," he crooned in her ear. He rubbed his stubbled jaw along the sensitive skin of her neck before his lips made a hot trail of their own.

She let out a happy sigh.

"We'd better eat before it gets cold," he said. "You're my dessert."

Their eyes met, and she found herself smiling like a fool. She shook her head and took a helping of potatoes and green beans and settled a plate on her lap too.

Ian cut into his turkey. "Welp, here goes nothing." He took a bite and chewed for a long time. "It's terrible. Mushy, chewy, and flavorless." He pointed his fork at her. "You're missing out."

She wrinkled her nose. "I don't even like turkey."

"Then why'd you make it?"

"I wanted to make you a traditional Christmas dinner. So you didn't feel like you were missing out from Christmas back home."

He cocked his head. "That's sweet, Kate. Thank you."

She flushed and dug into the potatoes, which were always her favorite. They were kinda hard, but she didn't think she could cook them anymore once they were mashed. The green beans were okay. Once they'd finished eating, Ian zonked out on the sofa.

She quietly cleared the food away, tucked the leftovers in the refrigerator, and called home. Barry answered. "Merry Christmas, Kate. We sure missed you and Ian, but I hope you're having a great time out there in Chicagoland."

"We are. We just finished dinner and now he's sleeping."

"Did you feed him turkey?"

"Yes."

"He always conks out after turkey." Then he said away from the phone, "It's Kate." There was a rustle and then she heard her sister.

"Hey!" Amber said. "Merry Christmas!" And then a little girl voice said, "Me-wy Tismas, Tate! I got doobie."

"Merry Christmas, Violet!" Kate exclaimed.

Amber got back on the phone. "She means her own paint set. I don't know why she calls it doobie. Why do you call it doobie, Vi?"

"Doobie doobie," Violet said in the background.

Amber laughed. "She's dancing. Maybe she means the music I play when I paint. How's it going with you and Ian?"

"Good. He's sleeping."

"So-o-oo?"

She smiled and gazed at Ian's sleeping form. "It's official. He's my boyfriend. We have a schedule for the long-distance arrangement, which is very satisfying."

"That's great! I know it's hard, but once you're finished out there…what is it? Only a year and a half, right? Then you won't have to be long distance. I hope you'll come back to the East Coast."

A trickling of unease went through her at the thought of the future. She didn't know where she'd be. There were a number of research facilities she was interested in both here and abroad. Would Ian be willing to move where her career took her? Or would he expect her to settle in Boston where he worked?

"I don't know," she whispered.

"Well, don't worry about that now," Amber said in a

reassuring tone. "Just play it by ear. I'm sure you'll work something out. Oh, your mom wants the phone."

Her parents had spent several holidays with Barry and Amber in order to visit their only grandchild. "Kate, we've missed you," her mom said.

"I missed you guys too," Kate replied.

"Is Chicago satisfactory?" her mom asked.

"Yes. I made Christmas dinner, but it didn't turn out very well."

"I hope you washed your hands after handling the turkey."

"I did. I know about salmonella."

There was a silence, and then she heard her dad's voice. "Merry Christmas, Kate. Too bad you got stuck out there."

"Yes. Merry Christmas to you too."

"How's Ian?"

"He's good."

"I'll see you when you come home again. When is that?"

"I don't know. I'll let you know as soon as I know."

"Okay. Your mother and I won't be spending the night here. Violet is too rambunctious in the morning, so I'll say goodbye now. We have to get back on the road." Her parents had a two-and-a-half-hour drive from Clover Park, Connecticut, back to Princeton, New Jersey. They both worked at Princeton University.

"Okay," Kate said. "Bye."

He hung up.

She snuggled up next to Ian on the sofa, and he stirred enough to pull her close, spooning her from behind. There was just no better place to feel loved than in his arms.

～

The morning after Christmas, Ian woke feeling nauseous. He ran to the bathroom and threw up. At first he thought nothing of it. Last night after his little nap, he and Kate had made eggnog. She had one drink and was immediately loopy. He tried the eggnog, thought it was gross, and switched to bourbon. More than he was used to. So he thought it was just that. But the queasy feeling didn't go away, and then he became one with the toilet. All day, coming out of both ends. It was awful.

He was so sick, and Kate kept her distance. He thought with some rancor between bouts of toilet bonding that she was the world's worst nurse. He'd probably die in this bathroom and she wouldn't know because she was on her laptop in the living room, catching up with whatever stupid physics equation had captured her interest.

He collapsed into bed as the sun was setting, dragging the bathroom trash can with him in case he threw up before he could make it back to the bathroom. "Water," he croaked.

No response.

"Kate!"

She appeared in the doorway. "What?"

"Can you get me some water?"

She turned and left. She returned, handed him the glass of water, and left. He took a sip. Then another. A few minutes later, he threw it all up. Fuck. He really was going to die here with Kate in the next room, completely oblivious to his suffering. She returned an hour later and offered him a slice of frozen pizza she'd heated up. The smell nauseated him, and he declined.

Hours later, he felt too weak to even yell for her. He snagged his cell off the nightstand and called her. "Please get in here," he said.

She appeared in the doorway. "What?"

"I can't keep anything down," he croaked. "Not even the water. I might need to go to the hospital."

"It's probably just the flu. Let's give it a couple of days. I'll sleep in the living room."

He collapsed into a deep sleep. He woke sick again in the middle of the night. It must've been that turkey, he thought dimly. Food poisoning. He'd eaten it. Kate hadn't. By the next morning he was still sick and so weak. His stomach muscles were killing him, cramping up painfully. He had nothing left in him, yet he couldn't stop running to the toilet.

Kate set a glass of water on the nightstand and eyed him where he lay miserably in bed. "I'm sure you'll be better by tomorrow."

She left. He sipped the water, and a few moments later, it all came up again.

He called Kate on his cell. "I need a doctor. I'm not getting better."

She appeared in the doorway. "Are you sure?"

She hadn't touched him since he got sick. He was pretty sure he was going to die on her watch. "I can't keep anything down, not even water."

She frowned. "The only doctor I know is Christopher, and he's in Wisconsin to spend Christmas with his family."

"Not him. There's got to be a doctor in Chicago that will give me something to make this stop."

"Did you have your flu shot? You should get one every year."

"No, I didn't get a flu shot," he said between his teeth.

She gave him a worried look. "I'm not sure if one will help at this point."

Nausea reared up, his stomach cramped, and he ran to the bathroom again. This was torture. Long horrific hours later, after another bout with the toilet, he washed his hands and took a staggering step toward the bedroom.

It was night, and he only hoped he could sleep straight through until morning. He was so exhausted. He took another staggering step, the room spun, and then he was falling, and the world went black.

Kate heard a loud thump from the bedroom shortly after a dinner of leftover pizza and found Ian collapsed on the floor. She pushed as hard as she could to roll him over. "Ian, wake up!" she shouted as panic raced through her. "Wake up!"

He wasn't responding. She slapped his cheek a few times. He was cold and clammy. With shaking hands, she grabbed her cell and called 911. She knew she couldn't lift him to get him into the car. The paramedics arrived: two men—one large, one small—and a woman. The large man, middle-aged with thinning brown hair and a no-nonsense expression, seemed to be in charge. She told them what happened and that she thought it was the flu. They checked Ian's vitals, his heart rate was high, and then they lifted him onto a gurney and strapped him on.

"And he's been sick like this for two days?" the paramedic in charge asked her.

"Yes," she choked out. Ian looked so weak and frail on the gurney. All six feet of him suddenly seemed fragile.

"He's severely dehydrated. You should've called sooner. This can be dangerous."

She watched as they put Ian into the ambulance, and she scrambled up behind him.

Ian opened his eyes. "What's happening?"

"You're going to the hospital," she told him.

His eyes drifted shut again. The ambulance raced toward the hospital, and she could do nothing but stare at Ian, lying there so cold and still, like death. The paramedic was asking him a question about his health history, and he wasn't responding.

She threw herself on top of him. "Don't die! I love you, I love you, I love you."

A sob escaped. And then another, and then she couldn't stop sobbing uncontrollably, soaking the thin blanket on top of him.

Ian's hand settled on the back of her head. "Hey," he croaked.

And then strong arms were pulling her away. She fought the paramedic pulling at her, but he was too strong. They asked Ian questions and ran an IV. As soon as the coast was clear, she went back to him, but he drifted into unconsciousness again. She couldn't stop crying, a low, keening sound interrupted by gasps of air.

"Calm down," the paramedic who wasn't in charge kept saying to her. "He's going to be fine."

But she didn't believe him. Not until Ian stayed conscious. Not until he was back, talking to her again. He drifted in and out of consciousness, occasionally mumbling something she couldn't make out. Finally, they arrived at the hospital.

"Are you his wife?" the paramedic in charge asked.

She sniffled. "No, I'm his girlfriend."

"You have to wait in the waiting room. Someone will come get you."

The doors of the ambulance opened, and she watched them take Ian away. She followed behind, stumbling along until she got to the waiting room, where he disappeared through the doors. She clapped a hand over her mouth, fighting another uncontrollable sob, and then she slid down the wall to the floor and broke down in tears. A nurse came and coaxed her to a chair. How had he gotten so sick so quickly? She'd looked up the flu online and it said it would pass on its own. She stood and paced for several minutes, watching the door for word on him. Then she couldn't take it anymore and took off after him.

"Hey!" a nurse said as she flew by.

"I'm his wife!"

After peeking through several curtains, she found him in one of the emergency room beds, where he was unconscious and alone. She looked at his kind face now drawn and pale, the face that she loved, and broke down all over again. She climbed into the hospital bed and hugged him tightly, sobbing all over his chest. "Ian, please wake up. I love you so much. So, so much. Please don't die. I love you, I love you, I love—"

"Kate." His voice rumbled in his chest.

Her head popped up. "Ian! You're alive."

"Yeah. What happened?"

"You collapsed. We're at the hospital, waiting for the doctor to come back, I think. I love you so much."

He licked his lips and tried to smile. "I heard that. I love you too. I'm so thirsty. My lips are dry."

She ripped the curtain back. "He needs water!"

A nurse with short-cropped brown hair nodded and headed over with a pitcher of water. "Just small sips."

"I'm so sorry you got so sick," she said.

Ian took a small sip of water and the nurse left. "I think it was the turkey."

"Not the flu?"

"No, because you're not sick from it. And you didn't have any turkey."

She flung her arms around him. "Omigod, this is all my fault. Me and my stupid Christmas dinner. I'm so sorry."

Ian pushed her away. "I still feel nauseous."

Kate leaped into action, standing in the middle of the emergency room. "We need a doctor! He's had food poisoning for two days! Someone take care of him!"

"A doctor will be with you shortly," the nurse that had helped them before said. The woman crossed to Ian's bed and looked at his chart. "He's already been seen. They gave him something to stop the vomiting and a doctor will follow up as soon as one's available."

The woman gave Kate a pointed look. "Please calm down. The ER is very busy today."

Kate scanned the room for a doctor. The nurse headed to the next patient.

"Ah, Kate," Ian said.

She rushed back to his side. "What?"

"Could you stop yelling and stay with me?"

"I'm trying to help you."

"I was so mad at you before for ignoring me when I was sick."

Her brows shot up. "But I gave you food and water. That's what my parents always did when I was sick."

"They left you alone with a cup of water?"

"Yes. You're supposed to stay away from the sick person, so you don't get it and spread it to others."

"Geez. You're lucky you never got that sick."

She thought about that. "I never did catch much. I didn't spend a lot of time with the other kids at school. I mostly studied." She bit her lip and fresh tears sprang to her eyes. "I'm sorry. I messed up. I didn't know what to do. I'm so sorry."

He took a deep breath. "If I survive this, I'm writing down instructions for you. How to take care of someone who's sick."

She sat by his side, grateful for his understanding. "Thank you, Ian."

"You're welcome," he muttered.

"I love you so much."

"Keep saying that. It makes me feel a little better. My stomach muscles hurt so bad." He put a hand to his stomach.

"I love you," she said. Then she left his side and stood in the middle of the emergency room and announced in a clear voice, "I need a doctor STAT. My husband is in terrible agony and it must stop." Not seeing a doctor racing to the rescue, she hollered at the top of her lungs, "Where's a doctor when you need one?"

A doctor finally appeared with a clipboard. "Lower your voice," the woman snapped. "We're extremely busy with a lot of patients and short on staff."

Kate pointed to Ian, who gave the doctor a weak wave.

Several hours later, Ian was released. The IV had hydrated him enough they felt they could return him to his wife's care. "Why'd you say you were my wife?" he asked once they'd settled into the backseat of a cab, heading back to her apartment.

"Because they wouldn't let me see you unless we were married."

He held her hand. "You think one day we will be?"

"I don't know." She had no idea what the future would hold, but right now she had to get some important information out of him. She dug a pencil and notepad out of her purse. She always kept them handy in case a break-through occurred to her away from the office. "Now tell me exactly what's expected of someone taking care of a recovering patient. Besides the doctor's instructions, rest and small sips of water and Gatorade." She repeated the doctor's instructions to make sure Ian knew he was in good hands now. "What else?"

"Number one. Rub my feet."

Kate wrote that down. "Because feet are connected to the circulatory system. Got it."

"Number two. Feed me grapes."

She wrote that down. "Are you sure? Maybe something blander like rice."

"Okay, feed me rice. Number three. Remain naked at all times."

She stopped and looked at him for the first time. He was grinning. "Ian! I need the real directions. You're not ending up in the hospital again!"

"That will help." He pointed to her notepad. "Write it down."

"It will not."

"Tell me again." He gazed warmly at her, and she knew what he wanted.

"I love you."

"Write that down for number four. And I love you too."

She wrote it down. "That's number three. The original three was false information."

"Number five," he said and waited until she looked up at him. Then he made an obscene gesture involving her mouth on him.

She put her pencil down. "Now I know you're feeling better."

"No thanks to you."

"I'm sorry! That's why I'm writing the instructions."

"Number five for real. Touch the patient. Hold their hand, hug them, stroke their hair. Anything."

She stilled. "What do you mean anything? Be specific."

"Okay, hold my hand and ask if I want food or water. Do not offer pizza to someone barfing up a lung. Try toast."

She wrote as fast as she could. "Food or water. Got it. No pizza. Toast recommended."

Ian leaned his head back on the seat. "You're lucky I love you so much."

"I know." She threw the notepad and pencil back in her purse and wrapped her arms around him.

He kissed her hair. "Do you realize that's the first time you hugged me first?"

"I hugged you a lot when I thought you were dead."

"That's reassuring."

"You're welcome."

He laughed and then clutched his stomach with a low groan.

Kate waited on Ian hand and foot for three more days, following his instructions to the letter. She knew he was feeling better when he suggested with a wink that the foot rub would work better if her hands traveled about three and a half feet higher. By New Year's Eve, Ian had made a full recovery and they were free to ring in the New Year in style. Ian surprised her with a purple tutu.

"When did you get this?" she exclaimed.

"When you were at work last week. I was hoping the blizzard would come through and we'd have New Year's together. Now you can be Cinderella at midnight."

She stared at the tutu. It wasn't exactly a ball gown. She felt a little silly.

"Put it on," he said. "It's part of my recovery."

"You're better already."

He snagged her by the loop of her jeans and stripped the jeans off for her. She pulled the tutu on. Then he pulled off her baggy sweater. "You match," he said.

She suddenly realized why he'd wanted her to wear her purple bra and panty set today. She normally wore plain white, but had a few different colored sets for the occasional time when she wanted to appeal to the opposite sex. He took her hand and twirled her around. The tutu spun out around her in a swishy way.

"Oh!" she exclaimed. She felt so light, almost transformed into a pretty ballerina.

He laughed. "Next time I'll get you a tiara to go with it."

"Don't be silly," she said, whirling and twirling again.

"Wait, you need music." He found the number two march from Tchaikovsky's *The Nutcracker* on his iPhone and played it. She'd never done ballet in her life, but found herself spinning and twirling like a ballerina. Ian occasionally joined in, helping her twirl and dipping her, which made her giggle madly.

"Happy New Year, Kate," he said when the song ended.

"Happy New Year," she said, wrapping her arms around his neck.

"To the first of many together," he said.

"Yes." She beamed. "I love you."

His brown eyes got shiny, which made her throat get tight. "I love you too."

Later, they watched the New Year ring in around the globe while she fed him grapes. Ian insisted they celebrate with champagne, which was delicious, and made her so lusty that they didn't even make it to the bedroom before she had him under her for their own explosive New Year's celebration. Kate had never been so happy in her life.

But the fun was over only two days later when Ian had to fly home.

Kate drove Ian to the airport, telling herself it wasn't really goodbye. Still, after their intense two weeks together, it was hard to let go. She pulled up to the curb for departures.

Ian turned to her and stroked her cheek. "This isn't the end, Kate."

She blinked rapidly. "I know. We'll have our HEA."

"Our what?"

She rolled her eyes. "Happy ever after!"

He grinned. "I like the sound of that."

His smile made her feel a little better. "Me too. This is more like our HFN."

"Happy forever nice?"

She blew out a breath. "Happy for now."

"I'm happy." He leaned close and kissed her. "I love you."

"I love you too." The words came shockingly easy to her now. Maybe it just took the right person to bring them out of her. She breathed in the scent of warm Ian and his woodsy, citrusy cologne, trying to hold onto the memory of it for later.

"Call me tonight for the scheduled phone sex," Ian said with a pointed look. It was Sunday night, not Friday night as they'd previously discussed, but she understood these were extreme circumstances.

"Already on my calendar." She gave him a dreamy smile and added, "We'll do it with the visual the first time. I'll wear my babydoll and you wear nothing. That will be helpful."

His large hand wrapped around the nape of her neck, and he kissed her again.

"You're a ten point five," she told him.

He smiled, his forehead touching hers. "You're off the charts."

"Oh, Ian. There's no such thing. You can always expand the data range. In fact, if you want to be accurate—"

He kissed her, long and deep, and her brain shut down, short-circuiting again. Only Ian could do that to her with one kiss.

He gazed at her tenderly and pulled back. "Bye for now."

"Bye," she choked out.

She watched him go and then drove home in her station wagon, grateful and so happy that she found a guy who truly understood her. More than anyone ever had, even her family. She decided then and there to plan a big surprise for him. He kept surprising her, which meant he must like surprises. That's what relationships were, a give and take, and thinking of what would make the other person happy. She hummed "Auld Lang Syne," knowing they'd meet up again soon.

Ian and Kate's story continues in *Almost Hitched*! They hit a few snags on the way to the wedding…

Almost Hitched

After a very satisfying long-distance relationship (following their very public relationship in *Almost Romance*), Kate Lewis and Ian Furnukle agree it's time to get hitched.

Except their jobs are thousands of miles apart.

And their trial run of living together didn't go so well.

And one of them has cold feet.

But that's nothing that true love (and some explosive chemistry) can't fix. If only love were a science.

Sign up for my newsletter and never miss a new release! https://www.kyliegilmore.com/newsletter

ALSO BY KYLIE GILMORE

Unleashed Romance <<steamy romcoms with dogs!

Fetching (Book 1)

Dashing (Book 2)

Sporting (Book 3)

Toying (Book 4)

Blazing (Book 5)

Chasing (Book 6)

Daring (Book 7)

Leading (Book 8)

Racing (Book 9)

Loving (Book 10)

The Clover Park Series <<brothers who put family first!

The Opposite of Wild (Book 1)

Daisy Does It All (Book 2)

Bad Taste in Men (Book 3)

Kissing Santa (Book 4)

Restless Harmony (Book 5)

Not My Romeo (Book 6)

Rev Me Up (Book 7)

An Ambitious Engagement (Book 8)

Clutch Player (Book 9)

A Tempting Friendship (Book 10)

Clover Park Bride: Nico and Lily's Wedding

A Valentine's Day Gift (Book 11)

Maggie Meets Her Match (Book 12)

The Clover Park Charmers series <<sweet and sexy charmers!

Almost Over It (Book 1)

Almost Married (Book 2)

Almost Fate (Book 3)

Almost in Love (Book 4)

Almost Romance (Book 5)

Almost Hitched (Book 6)

Happy Endings Book Club Series <<the Campbell family and a romance book club collide!

Hidden Hollywood (Book 1)

Inviting Trouble (Book 2)

So Revealing (Book 3)

Formal Arrangement (Book 4)

Bad Boy Done Wrong (Book 5)

Mess With Me (Book 6)

Resisting Fate (Book 7)

Chance of Romance (Book 8)

Wicked Flirt (Book 9)

An Inconvenient Plan (Book 10)

A Happy Endings Wedding (Book 11)

The Rourkes Series <<swoonworthy princes and kickass princesses!

Royal Catch (Book 1)

Royal Hottie (Book 2)

Royal Darling (Book 3)

Royal Charmer (Book 4)

Royal Player (Book 5)

Royal Shark (Book 6)

Rogue Prince (Book 7)

Rogue Gentleman (Book 8)

Rogue Rascal (Book 9)

Rogue Angel (Book 10)

Rogue Devil (Book 11)

Rogue Beast (Book 12)

Check out my website for the most up-to-date list of my books: kyliegilmore.com/books

ABOUT THE AUTHOR

Kylie Gilmore is the *USA Today* bestselling author of over fifty humorous contemporary romances. Her series include Unleashed Romance, the Rourkes, the Happy Endings Book Club, Clover Park, and Clover Park Charmers. With more than three million downloads of her books, readers all over the world love escaping into her hilarious feel-good romances featuring strong bonds with family, friends, and community.

Kylie lives in New York with her family, a demanding cat, and a nutso dog. When she's not writing, reading hot romance, or dutifully taking notes at writing conferences, you can find her flexing her muscles all the way to the high cabinet for her secret chocolate stash.

Sign up for Kylie's Newsletter and get a FREE book! kyliegilmore.com/newsletter

For text alerts on Kylie's new releases, text KYLIE to the number (888) 707-3025. (US only)

For more fun stuff check out Kylie's website https://www.kyliegilmore.com.

Thanks for reading *Almost Romance*. I hope you enjoyed it. Would you like to know about new releases? You can sign up for my new release email list at kyliegilmore.com/newsletter. I promise not to clog your inbox! Only new release info, sales, and some fun giveaways.

I love to hear from readers! You can find me at:
  kyliegilmore.com
  Facebook.com/KylieGilmoreToo
  Twitter @KylieGilmoreToo

If you liked Ian and Kate's story, please leave a review on your favorite retailer's website or Goodreads. Thank you.